the Undrowned

the Undrowned

K. R. Alexander

Scholastic Inc.

Copyright © 2020 by Alex R. Kahler writing as K. R. Alexander

All rights reserved. Published by Scholastic Inc., *Publishers since 1920*. SCHOLASTIC and associated logos are trademarks and/or registered trademarks of Scholastic Inc.

The publisher does not have any control over and does not assume any responsibility for author or third-party websites or their content.

No part of this publication may be reproduced, stored in a retrieval system, or transmitted in any form or by any means, electronic, mechanical, photocopying, recording, or otherwise, without written permission of the publisher. For information regarding permission, write to Scholastic Inc., Attention: Permissions Department, 557 Broadway, New York, NY 10012.

This book is a work of fiction. Names, characters, places, and incidents are either the product of the author's imagination or are used fictitiously, and any resemblance to actual persons, living or dead, business establishments, events, or locales is entirely coincidental.

ISBN 978-1-338-54052-9

10 9 8 7 6 5 4 3 2 1   20 21 22 23 24

Printed in the U.S.A.   40
First printing 2020

Book design by Baily Crawford

For those unafraid to face
their demons

The dead don't come back.

When I was a little girl, maybe four or five, I remember my mom patiently explaining this to me as we buried my pet hamster in the backyard. I was crying, because I was confused. Why was NomNom sleeping for so long? Why wasn't he waking up? Why had my mom insisted we make him a cute bed of paper towels and spare fabric and flowers and bury him in a shoebox by the daffodils? How could he see? How could he *breathe*?

"You see, Samantha," Mom said, "sometimes when animals get very sick or very old, they go to sleep and never wake up again."

"Never?" I asked, sniffling.

"Never." She took my hand, and together we said goodbye to NomNom and began to shovel dirt on top of him. I still didn't know *why* we were saying goodbye. I still didn't understand how something could sleep forever. Even when *I* was really tired, I woke up eventually.

"But what if he's different?" I asked. "What if he's really just sleeping?"

"He's not coming back, pumpkin. He's dead now. The dead don't come back."

I swallowed, and things clicked far too quickly in my too-young brain.

"Do people die, too?" I asked.

She paused. I remember the way she looked at me, like she was trying to figure out whether or not to tell me the truth. I could feel myself teetering on the edge of something vast and terrifying in that moment, and her answer would either pull me back to safety or push me over the edge.

"Yes," she finally said. "People die, too. And just like NomNom, they don't come back."

I thought for years that she'd decided to tell me the truth.

Only now am I realizing that it was a lie.

Because when I pushed Rachel into the lake and she didn't come back up, I knew she was dead. She wasn't coming back.

Except, the next day, she did.

1

Wednesday is *not* going my way, and I know just who is going to pay for it.

I still have my parents' argument ringing in my ears when I get to school. All morning they've been fighting. Not just about each other and how they both *work too much*, which is what they usually spend breakfast fighting about, but because I failed a spelling test.

One stupid spelling test.

Now they're refusing to take me on a day trip to Rocky River Adventure Park this Saturday like they promised, all because I misspelled a few words like *possessed* and *allegory*. (Who needs to know how to spell those, anyway? I always have my phone, and that can fix spelling for me. As if I'd ever even use any of the spelling words in the first place.)

So, no theme park for me. My so-called friends will still be going, because *their* parents aren't jerks like mine. And I'm sure I'll hear all about how amazing it was on Monday.

All I get to look forward to is a weekend of doing homework while my parents continue to argue downstairs and my sister plays video games with her friends, and none of it's fair because it's not really my fault that I didn't have time to study for the spelling test. I'd been too busy writing the essay that Rachel was supposed to do for me. She let me down. Again.

It's her fault.

All of this is her fault.

And I'm going to make sure it's the last time.

I stomp through the school's front doors and down the hallway, and it must be pretty clear that I'm angry—kids actually step away from me, parting and going quiet so I can pass, hoping they won't be the latest victims of my wrath. I shove past a few of them. Knock books out of a nerd's hands, slam another kid into his friend. No different from my normal entrance.

But the truth is, I barely even see them. They're not worth my time, let alone my anger.

Rachel is.

I see her at her locker before she ever sees me. Short and pretty, with long black hair and perfect skin and big blue eyes. I'm tall and have the same black hair, but my skin is far from perfect, which some kids used to make fun of me for, until I started pushing back and proving I wasn't someone you could make fun of. Now the only bully in this school is *me*.

"You," I growl when I reach her locker. I slam it shut to emphasize my point.

She jumps back with a yelp and clutches her sketchbook to her chest with both hands, eyes wide and lip already quivering like a baby's. She knows when I'm in a bad mood, and it's clear she knows this is worse than all the rest.

"I—"

"Shut up," I say. "Do you have any idea what you've done?"

"I—I—" she stutters.

"Because of you and your stupid little pea-brain, my parents aren't taking me to the adventure park this weekend. You were supposed to write my essay, but you didn't, and because of that I couldn't study for the spelling test. It's your fault I failed. And you're going to pay for it."

I want to shove her against the locker, but I hold myself back. Partly because I know she'd just start crying and partly because I see our principal, Mr. Detmer, out of the corner of my eye. He's watching us. I don't need to get detention again—the last thing I need is to be grounded.

I lower my voice.

"I'm going to get you back for this." I look into her eyes, and she looks to her feet. "If I have to suffer, so will you. Now, hand it over."

She nods. She doesn't ask what I want or what I mean. She already knows.

We have this down to an art. Almost a symbiotic relationship—a situation where both parties benefit from the other's skills. I learned that term in science.

In this case, it means I don't beat her up, and she does my homework and pays for my lunch.

It wasn't always like this with us.

We used to be friends. Best friends.

Used to.

I can't even really imagine it anymore. I guess we were friends when we were both younger. Weaker.

Now I'm no longer weak; she taught me that friendship is the ultimate weakness. Friends can hurt you. Friends can make your whole life miserable if they know everything about you. And from her betrayal, I grew strong. I used that lesson against her, because she deserved all that and more.

Am I using her?

Sure.

But it's the only use she has in our school. Otherwise, she's nothing. I make sure of it.

She opens her locker again—which takes a second, since she has to reenter her code—and pulls out a folder. I flip it open and check, but she hasn't disappointed me on this, at least. She knows not to let me down again. The social studies homework we got yesterday is done, along with the math practice sheets. And there, in the front pocket, is the five dollars she gives me every day for lunch.

I've never asked where she gets the money. Probably her parents. They're loaded. They even have a pool in their backyard. Perfect Rachel and her perfect life. Her perfectly useless life.

She could give me a million dollars, and she'd still owe me.

I snap the folder shut and slam her locker closed again.

I miss her fingers. Barely.

Gotta keep her a little scared. Tears well in her eyes.

I don't say anything when I turn and stomp down the hall to my locker. I shove into another kid on the way, making her drop her bag, her books and homework scattering all over the floor. Mr. Detmer calls out to me, but I'm already around the corner, and I know he won't follow.

He's a little scared of me, too.

He should be.

They all should be.

2

I manage to get through all my classes without getting a detention, even though a part of me really just wants to explode. It doesn't help that at lunch, the few friends I keep around spend the whole time talking about the rides they're excited to go on this weekend. Neither Felicia nor Sarah asks why I don't say anything. When I finally blurt out that I'm not going, and could they just shut up about it, I think they honestly look relieved that I won't be there. It definitely doesn't improve my mood, but whatever.

I don't need them.

I don't need any of them.

Friendship. Is. Weakness.

It makes me glance over to Rachel, who sits on her own at the far end of a corner table, face down in her sketchbook like usual. Years ago, *we* would be going to the adventure park together, no questions asked. We had many times before. Until she ruined everything by betraying me.

A small part of me wonders what she's writing in her journal—wonders if she's writing about *me*—but I don't think she'd do that again.

She learned the hard way what happens when she writes mean things behind my back.

I push her out of my mind. She could disappear for all I care.

I wish I could *make* her disappear.

At the end of the day we have a pop quiz in science class that I'm pretty certain I fail because I'm too angry at Sarah and Felicia to focus. By the end of lunch, they hadn't even asked *why* I wasn't going to the park. It's like they didn't even care!

Whatever. I don't care about them, either. I only

have a year left at this boring middle school, and then I can make new friends. Better friends.

No, friends just leave or hurt you in the end. I need to get to a point where I don't need anybody.

The only person I'll keep around is Rachel. So I can keep making her life miserable, and so she can do my homework for me.

But when I leave my last class to give my homework to Rachel, she isn't at her locker.

That, more than anything, makes me angry.

She knows she's supposed to wait for me.

She knows her *place*.

I slam my fist against her locker and storm off.

I don't go home.

Lately I want to spend less and less time there. My parents are always busy, and although my dad works in an office, Mom works from home. When they *are* home together, they basically yell at each other about always being too busy for quality time, whatever that means. And sometimes they turn their anger at each other toward me. I might have everyone at school—including the teachers—scared of me (last year I even managed to get a lunch lady fired by hiding thumbtacks in my lasagna and saying I'd overheard her muttering that she hated my guts). But home is a different story. The complete opposite.

They yell at me for every bad grade.

Ground me for every detention.

Take away my desserts, my TV time, my phone. Once, they even tried sending me to a counselor for anger management, until I threw a hunger strike and they caved.

And honestly, I might not even mind all that, because whatever, I get over it—but every time I do something that makes my parents say they're *ashamed* of me, they compare me to my sister.

My perfect, stupid little sister and her perfect grades and perfect attitude. A constant reminder that I'm not good enough.

Just like Rachel.

My sister, Jessica, is too much of a goody-two-shoes to do anything wrong, which means everyone always trusts and believes her; if I break a single rule at home or try to hide something I did at school, she finds out and tells Mom or Dad. And Mom is *always* on the edge of a screaming fit. Jessica knows it. She's basically the only person in the world I can't bully, because all I have to do is look at her funny and she cries to our parents and I get grounded or worse. No doubt she'd try to get me in trouble if I came home and did anything besides my homework, and right now, homework is the last thing I want to do.

All I want to do is yell at someone or punch something or run around because *this isn't fair.*

It's not fair, and about the only thing I can do about it is try to avoid going home like the plague. So I wander.

Roseboro is small and boring and I hate it. As I storm down the sidewalk, past the houses I've seen literally every day of my entire life, my anger builds. Not just because of Rachel or my parents or missing the theme park, but because I am *bored.* There's nothing to do around here. About the only fun thing is Rocky River Adventure Park, and even that's mostly for little kids and half an hour away. It's not fair. I'm going to be bored all weekend, just like I'm bored every other day.

Why couldn't we live somewhere cool, like Seattle or New York or LA? A place where things actually *happen* and there's more to do than go to the diner for milkshakes after school or stay at home and stream countless shows and movies. Somewhere with *cool* people who do *cool* things. *That's* where I belong. Among movie stars and popular kids who know that the only way to get to the top is to beat your way there.

Yeah. I'd fit in perfectly somewhere like that.

I'm so wrapped up in my head that I don't even realize I've taken the *really* long way home. Past the main streets, around all the suburbs, and out into the woods and fields that stretch out on all sides of our town, ensuring that nothing cool or urban ever makes its way here. It would have to push through too much corn.

For a split second I consider turning around. Even though it's sunny and a while until sunset, I know better than to be alone in the woods. I'm not worried about monsters or anything childish like that. I just know that sometimes creepy people prowl the forest. Or at least that's what my mom said when I'd been out playing in a park by myself after dark. Later that week, as if to emphasize her point, the news reported that a little kid had gone missing, presumably drowned in Lake Lamont.

They never caught a killer.

Not that I'm scared in the slightest. A small part of me *wants* to run into a creepy stranger. At least then I'll have someone to vent all my anger toward. Then the police would be totally okay with me beating someone up. I might even get a medal.

That would show everyone.

The path through the woods twists and turns, finally coming to a fork. One way leads back to town, the other to Lake Lamont.

I've heard so many stories about the lake, and even though I've been there many times, a part of me always wonders if the stories are true.

Kids drowning,

bodies going missing,

strange sounds or lights at night.

It's probably just rumors told by teens to scare off younger kids so they can have the lake to themselves.

Still, there's a voice inside me that whispers not to go there, a voice that sounds a lot like my mom's.

That's what does it. If *she* doesn't want me to go there, then *I* do.

I head toward the lake.

And surprise, surprise, when the lake comes into view, I realize I'm not the only one there.

3

I can't tell if my luck is improving or taking a downturn.

There, sitting at the far end of a dock that juts into the middle of the large lake, drawing in her stupid sketchbook, is Rachel.

My veins turn to acid at the sight of her. My vision narrows.

Everything wrong in my life feels like it's her fault.

My parents fighting.

My bad grades.

My bad mood.

Being stuck in this tiny town with no one to turn to,

no one to help make the dullness manageable. Once I see her, all the anger and rage that had been building over the day boil up to the surface.

"What the heck are you doing here?" I yell out.

My voice echoes across the lake, causing a flock of birds to scream out and fly away. Rachel startles and drops her pen in the water. When she sees me, she grabs her sketchbook and holds it tight to her chest, staring at me with her eyes wide, like a cornered rabbit looking for escape.

But it's easy to see there *is* no escape. The lake is the size of five city blocks and trees tower up on all sides. There are docks on the far side where rich people keep their boats. But here, on our side, we are alone. Completely alone.

Since she is out on the pier, the only way past me would be to swim.

And we both know she never learned how to swim.

Every time she tried, she failed.

Every time she tried, she had to be saved. By me.

And I'm definitely not saving her this time.

"Samantha," she says. Her voice quavers. She doesn't

say anything else, but the question is there in her tone: *What are you doing here?*

Or, most likely: *What are you going to do to me?*

It's a good thing she doesn't actually ask, because I don't have an answer.

And if I had to come up with one, I'm sure she wouldn't like it.

I drop my backpack on the grass and stomp toward her. My feet echo on the wooden planks when I reach the docks—a battle march. Rachel sets down her sketchbook and stands up, stepping in front of the book like she's trying to protect it from me. I don't care what she's writing in there. Probably some stupid poems or sad drawings.

It must suck to be her.

But I

            don't

                    care.

I want to curse at her, but I can't find the words. Rage has formed a knot in my throat. But that's okay, because we are far past talking.

Now that I'm here, now that I see her, there's a part of me that feels like I was meant to be here all along.

And that part of me overflows with anger. It takes me over like an otherworldly force. The rage is outside my control. It wants to hurt someone. Badly.

She is absolutely terrified of me, and I'm even mad at her for that. Because even this anger is her fault.

"Samantha," she snivels, "I'm so sorry I forgot about the essay. My hamster died and I—"

My memory flashes, and for a brief moment I am back in my backyard with my mom at my side, tears in my eyes as we turned away from NomNom for the last time. Then I blink, and I'm back, and I'm somehow angrier than ever.

"I don't care about your stupid dead hamster!" I shout. "It's your fault. All of this is your fault!"

She cowers. "I'm sorry," she says, her words trembling. "I'm so sorry I—"

"I don't care about sorry, either!" I yell back.

I don't want her to be sorry.

I want her to fight back.

I want her to yell at me and tell me I'm wrong, to justify my anger with her own. But she just stands there, looking at me like I've turned into a monster, unwilling to fight. She bows her head, just a little, and I know I won't get a battle out of her.

At least, not like this.

I push her.

Just a little shove. Enough to make her gasp and wobble.

"Come on," I taunt. "Fight back. You know you want to. You know you want to hurt me. You've always wanted to hurt me. Even more than you already have."

"I'm not going to fight you," Rachel says. "I'm sorry I hurt you before. We don't need to fight. We don't—"

"Oh, we're going to fight," I say, then push her again. "I've had it with you, Rachel. It's your fault I'm failing. Your fault I'm not going to the adventure park. Your fault my parents—" I cut off. She doesn't know about my parents fighting, and she's not going to.

"I'm sorry," she says again. So softly, almost soothing, like she's trying to calm an angry dog.

It makes me hate her even more.

I push her again. A little harder this time. She takes a step back to right herself.

Her foot is only a couple steps from the edge of the pier.

"You're sorry?" I yell. "Sorry isn't good enough, Rachel! *Sorry*—"

I tap her shoulder

"*isn't*—"

I push her other shoulder

"*enough!*"

I shove both her shoulders. Harder than either of us expects.

She stumbles backward, arms cartwheeling for balance.

One step.

Two steps.

No—

Her wide eyes lock onto mine, and that one glance is almost enough to quell my rage.

I have never seen her that terrified before.

Splash!

She falls backward into the lake before I can reach out to stop her—and I stand there, watching the waves ripple. Watching the slight foam. My breath heaves in my chest and my blood is so hot I feel like I'm going to burst.

That same small voice from before tells me I should help her.

I don't.

She'll be fine.

It's not even that deep.

I wait for her to surface. Already, my anger is turning to humor. She's going to have to walk home sopping wet. Her clothes will be *ruined*. That, at least, will make up for the mess she's made of my life. I laugh at the thought.

Yes. I stand there and laugh.

Twenty seconds pass.

The water stills.

My humor starts to fade.

Thirty.

No more waves. No more bubbles.

Forty.

"Rachel?" I whisper.

Sixty.

Seventy.

I look around the lake, thinking maybe she surfaced near the shore. But everything is still and silent.

Everything is waiting.

I wait, too.

Three minutes pass, and when I hit one hundred and eighty seconds, I know there's no point waiting anymore.

4

I know I should try to help her.

My mom's voice is screaming in my head to go find help. Call 911. Grab a stick and reach in and try to fish her out.

Or jump in.

Swim.

Dive.

Find her in the seaweed.

I know how to swim.

Rachel doesn't.

I should be trying to help her. I should be trying to save her life.

But I am frozen at the edge of the dock.

Frozen by fear. And by something else. Something I can't quite place.

Like the rage before, a calm settles over me.

Immobilizes me.

Soothes and stills my mother's rational voice inside. It's okay. It's all okay.

This is precisely what I wanted to happen.

Precisely what was *supposed* to happen.

I don't know how long I stand at the edge of the pier.

Waiting for Rachel to surface, even though I know she won't be surfacing by now. No one can hold their breath that long. Especially not her.

I stare out over the crystalline waters, at the clear blue sky, and for the first time all day, I feel—horrible as it may sound—at peace.

Rachel is gone.

And since she was the reason my life was bad, that means my problems have to be gone as well.

I look down and see the sketchbook still on the edge of the dock. It teeters on the corner, just about to fall in.

The sight of it brings me back to motion; I lean over and grab it.

The moment I touch the water-flecked cover, my calm fades.

Reality sinks in.

Rachel isn't coming back.

I've killed her.

I'm a murderer.

Quickly, I glance around, but there's no one else in the woods or by the lake, no one who would have seen what happened.

No one knows.

No one knows that she was here.

No one knows that I was here.

I need to keep it that way.

At that moment, as panic starts racing through me, the only thing I can think of is getting out of here before someone walks out of the woods and discovers me. Starts asking questions.

I take one last look around at the placid lake, then run to my backpack and shove the sketchbook inside. I don't pause or look back.

I keep running, and I don't stop until I leave the woods.

Rachel is dead.

She isn't coming back.

And no one knows it but me.

5

"Are you feeling okay?" my sister, Jessica, asks. "You look like you're getting sick."

I glare over at her as I push mushy carrots around on my plate. I don't answer her, because any answer I give would be rude, and I need to fly under the radar right now.

This is the point where my parents are supposed to look over with concern on their faces and check my temperature or something. But they don't, because my mom is eating in her home office and my dad is reading something on his phone.

Another normal, happy family meal.

I haven't said anything all night. Which isn't that strange, really, because none of us talk during dinner. But I *feel* sick, and I can't bring myself to eat anything. My stomach is in knots; eating is the last thing on my mind.

It's hitting me then that I should have run home and pretended that I'd been there all along so Jessica would be able to back me up if anyone asked. It would have been easy enough to do—she never pays attention when I come home, anyway.

Stupid, I yell at myself. It's too late to do it now without calling too much attention to myself. I can always ask her to back me up later if I have to. Though I doubt that would work; if she knew it involved breaking the law, she'd rat me out faster than I could blink.

I keep waiting for the phone to ring.

Or for Dad to get a text from Rachel's concerned parents.

Some kind of message.

Some kind of news.

Rachel is missing, have you seen her?

Finally, when it's clear that I'm not going to actually eat anything tonight, I excuse myself and toss my food in the compost before running upstairs.

Thankfully, no one asks where I'm going or what I'm doing. No one cares.

It's probably the first time I've felt thankful about that.

I rush up to my room and lock the door behind me.

My room is a mess, but I don't care. Clothes in the corner beside the hamper, old toys and things I don't play with anymore piling up in my closet, a few trophies from when I actually cared about stupid things like school and sports. My mom used to get on my case about keeping things tidy, but that was a while ago, before she and my dad started really fighting. Which is good, because I currently have Rachel's sketchbook shoved under my dirty laundry. No one would dare look in there.

I switch on my laptop and immediately go to the local news. I even turn on the TV on my bureau and flip it to the news as well. Then, even though I don't know how I'm going to focus, I grab my pile of homework and try to slog my way through while the news mumbles quietly in the background. I'm definitely focused on what the anchors are saying more than the questions on the page. But I need to at least try to get this done. I don't need any more trouble at home.

I keep glancing at the pile of clothes. Like I'm worried it's going to move or Rachel's sketchbook is going to jump out and start screaming *SHE DID IT, SHE MURDERED ME!*

But of course that doesn't happen. It doesn't help my nerves any, though.

Especially because the news doesn't tell me a thing.

There are the usual stories, sure, but nothing about a missing girl. I scour the Internet and keep looking at the live news.

Nothing.

It makes my skin crawl.

Maybe Rachel's parents haven't reported her missing yet.

Maybe no one's been to the lake since we were there.

Maybe her body sank. Maybe she'll never be found.

Maybe her parents will think she ran away.

Maybe I'll get away with it.

The thought feels dangerous. I can't let my guard down. There's no way I can get away with it this easily.

There's no way you should *get away with this so easily.* It's my mother's voice, and I know she's right.

Now that I'm here, alone, my adrenaline starts to fade. The anger I felt earlier melts. Just enough that I start to fully realize what I've done.

I've killed someone.

I always knew I was a bad person, but I never thought I was a *horrible* person.

Not like this.

But it was an accident! I remind myself, over and over.

It was an accident.

It was an accident.

I didn't mean to kill her.

I only wanted to scare her.

To make fun of her.

I'd never actually hurt her.

Not really.

Not like that.

   But you would, a cruel voice inside me whispers. *You have, and you would. And you would do it again.*

Someone is going to find out. Someone is going to trace it back to me.

I blink, and a tear drops down to my laptop keyboard.

The trouble is, I can't tell who or what I'm crying for.

For the girl whose life I ended?

Or for me?

Because now I know that my life is over, too.

6

I dream of drowning.

I thrash against the long strands of seaweed that twine around my ankles and wrists, but it's no good. Every time I move, they twist tighter. Bubbles rise from my nostrils and float slowly toward the surface glittering brightly above. My lungs burn.

I have to get out of here.

I have to get free.

I struggle harder, trying to rip out the seaweed—and it's then that I realize there are more than plants down here.

There are other shapes trapped by the seaweed.

At first, I think they are dolls. Or mannequins.

Then one turns to me, eyes and mouth wide open in a long-silenced scream.

Rachel.

I scream as well, my world exploding into bubbles. And as the final bits of air leave me, I feel the seaweed dragging me down.

Deeper into the lake.

Deeper amidst the bodies.

Deeper, to the place where my darkest secrets have drowned.

7

When I wake up I am covered in sweat. For a moment, I wonder if maybe Jessica was right and I really *am* sick. But then a few minutes pass and my pulse slows and my dream comes back into focus.

I'm not sick. I'm still reeling from the nightmares.

A part of me considers pretending to be sick. Staying home. It wouldn't be that much of a lie, anyway: The idea of going to school and pretending that everything is okay makes me sick to my stomach.

Rachel's parents have to be panicking by now. Even if they don't know she's dead, they know she's missing. And that kind of news will travel fast. The school will be a chaos of rumors and questions. I can see it now—kids crying and hugging in the halls because one of their classmates is missing, teachers scared because they think a killer is on the loose—and they'd be right, though the killer wouldn't be some mysterious stranger. The killer would be wandering the halls with them.

Worse, I'm sure there will be cops there.

We'll be questioned.

They'll want to know who saw Rachel last. Or if anyone would want to hurt her. And everyone will point at me and say that I've been bullying her for years.

They'll say if anyone is a suspect, it's me.

This makes me want to stay home even more. But I realize that staying home would seem awfully suspicious. If the cops came here to question me and realized I was lying about being sick, they might think I'm lying about Rachel, too.

I can't risk it.

Even though it's the absolute last thing I want to do, I roll out of bed and start to get ready. I feel like a zombie even after I shower, and nearly stumble down the steps on my way to breakfast.

Jessica notices.

"Didn't sleep?" she asks me. There's a textbook beside the cereal bowl in front of her. Not because she's cramming last minute like I would have done, but because she probably just wants to make extra sure that she knows everything. Because she always knows everything. Even, apparently, when I'm not sleeping.

"Bad dreams," I mutter, and even that feels too close to the truth. I expect her to ask what they were about, but she just grunts and goes back to her reading.

I go to the cabinet to grab my own bowl when Mom comes in. She works as an interior designer, so she's almost always home unless she's out with a client. Most of the time she just ignores us, and I try to avoid eye contact so she'll do just that. But my luck today has already run out.

"Did you get all your homework done?" Mom asks.

I stall.

"Um . . ."

"Samantha Jean," she says, her voice taking on the stern tone I've grown to fear. "If I get one more note from your teachers that you're failing a class, we are going to have a discussion."

Discussion, I know, is code for *yelling at you for hours and grounding you until you're eighteen.*

"I got it done!" I say. It's not a lie. Not really. I finished all my homework—I just don't know if I did it *well*. I couldn't focus with worries of Rachel running through my head.

Mom looks me in the eye. Her eyes are about as fierce as her tone.

"If I find out you're lying," she warns.

"I'm not." I lower my gaze. I don't want her to notice anything else in my expression, don't want her asking why I look like I haven't slept.

"Why couldn't you be more like your sister?" she asks with a sigh and goes over to kiss Jessica on the top of her head.

Jessica, at least, doesn't look proud of the attention. She just buries herself in her textbook.

"I expect a passing grade from you this semester," Mom says as she pours more coffee for herself. "If you don't start applying yourself now, you won't get anywhere in life. And I refuse to have a failure as a daughter."

That stings. I hold the empty bowl so tight I expect it to shatter in my hands. Mom stomps out.

"She didn't mean it," Jessica whispers. I turn around to see her staring at me nervously.

"Yes," I say, fighting back the tears. "She did."

"I—"

"Shut up, Jessica," I say.

Thankfully, she does.

I pour myself some cereal even though eating is the last thing on my mind, then sit at the table as far from my sister as possible.

The TV is playing in the other room. Dad has the news on before he heads to the office. I keep my ears peeled but try not to seem interested. I don't hear anything about a missing kid. I don't hear Rachel's name. And when I trudge back upstairs to grab my things, I check the Internet one more time.

Nothing.

How has no one reported this yet? How has no one found her body? Why haven't her parents called her in as missing?

The complete lack of coverage has me on edge.

If they already know what you did, there's no need to announce it. They're probably on their way here now.

I delete my browser history so no one can wonder why I was looking at the news in the first place.

I'm just about to leave my room when I have an idea that sends chills down my spine.

It would be just my luck that Mom would pick today to be a good parent and clean my room for me during one of her work breaks. But there's no time to find a safer place. Still, I run to the dirty clothes and reach into the pile, just to make sure I hid it properly. Just to make sure it's still there. My hands close around the sketchbook.

I tell myself it's my imagination, or maybe a leaking water bottle, but I swear that the sketchbook feels wet.

8

I feel sick the entire way to school.

Not just nervous. No, this is way beyond nervous. Every few steps I have to pause and tell myself to stop being ridiculous, to stop looking scared, and to stop feeling like I'm about to throw up. I keep looking around, waiting for a cop car to whiz past on its way to the school or pull up behind me with its lights and sirens blaring. I watch the faces of the kids who walk along the street with me. They all look away—they know not to mess with me—but they don't look sad. No one is crying or looking more scared than usual.

That almost makes my stomach feel worse. It might be calm out here, but I bet anything that the school will be in full panic mode.

Except . . . when I get to school, it doesn't seem any different from before. There are kids milling about out front and talking and even laughing. Don't they know that Rachel is missing? That she might be dead? There is a murderer walking among them right now.

(But it was an accident. It was an accident.)

No one looks at me twice when I make my way up to the big double doors. No one whispers secrets behind my back. They just move out of my way like they always do.

Everything feels completely normal, and that feels completely wrong. Should I slam someone against their locker? Should I knock the homework out of that kid's hands? I don't want to look suspicious, but I don't want to draw attention to myself, either.

I settle on glaring at anyone who looks at me, making them avert their eyes or run away.

It's hard to keep my angry composure. I can't stop thinking about how much trouble I'm in.

At the very least, there should be signs posted about a missing girl. Right?

A wave of nausea crashes within me and I stumble, grabbing on to the door to stay upright. Maybe I should go home. This was a bad idea. A really bad idea. Even if it means facing the inevitable questions and wrath of my mother, it has to be better than this.

I'm going to crack. I know it.

Someone walks into me. A girl the grade below me.

"Sorry!" she squeaks. She flinches when I look at her. Expects me to scream and yell, and I know I've screamed at her before.

"It's fine," I manage.

Her eyebrows furrow, but she doesn't say anything about my strange behavior, just turns and scurries off.

Pull yourself together, Samantha. You have to be mean. You can't look suspicious.

I can do this.

I don't have a choice.

No one else seems to care about my presence as I walk down the hall. There's no commotion in here, no panic or tears. Kids wander and laugh just like they did outside. There aren't any cops questioning kids on when they last saw Rachel or who she was with. No newspaper reporters interviewing teachers or students to learn more about her story.

It's just a normal Thursday.

Everyone seems bubblier and louder now that it's almost the weekend. Everyone seems happy and completely unaware of the monster in their midst.

Once again, the normalcy makes me feel worse. Because the news *will* drop soon that Rachel is either missing or dead. I don't want to spend all day on edge waiting for it to happen. I almost want to run down the hallway screaming at the top of my lungs, *"Don't you all realize she's gone? Why don't you seem to care? Rachel is missing! Rachel is dead!"*

I don't do that, though. Even if the idea does take over my thoughts as I near my locker. Even if I'm equally torn between running home or running down the halls screaming. I may be freaking out, but I haven't gone crazy. Not yet.

My heart somewhere in my throat, I begin to gather my things. Already, the daily routine feels off—this is when I should be trying to find Rachel and demanding she give me my homework and lunch money. The thought makes me feel bad, and that's dangerous.

I can't. Feel. Guilty.

Otherwise I will be found out for sure.

When I slam my locker shut, I catch sight of someone passing around the corner and nearly gasp.

It can't be.

Long black hair. That familiar blue polka-dot top.

No way.

My blood goes cold as I slowly walk toward the hall. Everything else in the school seems muted, conversation and laughter dulled down to the low sound of rushing water.

I turn the corner.

There, by her locker as usual, is Rachel.

I gasp and leap behind the corner, pressing my back up against the lockers and breathing heavily. My heart thuds so loud in my chest I can barely hear the two words hammering on repeat in my head.

No way.

No way no way no way.

It can't be Rachel.
I saw her drown.
Or at least I thought I did.

Did she survive?

The thought should fill me with relief, but instead it terrifies me.

Because if she's alive, she'll tell someone that I pushed her.

That I didn't try to save her.

That I left her there to drown and didn't tell anyone, like a true criminal.

How did she make it out alive? I never saw her come back up, and I know I stayed on the dock far longer than anyone can hold their breath. Did she secretly swim to the shore and sneak out without me noticing? Did she watch me and laugh at me while I panicked? Was it all some sort of creepy test or torture?

Slowly, I peek my head back around the corner.

It's her. It's definitely her. The long black hair and blue shirt I got her for her birthday when we were still friends, the perfect skin and pale blue eyes.

I swallow heavily, trying to breathe slowly and regularly, as I watch her put her backpack away and gather her books.

Her books! I still have her sketchbook. Is she going to use that against me somehow?

Even though there are dozens of kids walking around or between us, it feels like it's just her and me in the hall. Her and me, and she still hasn't realized I'm here, watching.

I have to keep it that way. She can't see me. If she does, she'll confront me. She'll scream at the top of her lungs that I tried to kill her. She'll call all the teachers and they'll call the cops and I will go to jail.

If she sees me, I know I am done for. If I run home, it will be highly suspicious. The only thing I can do is try to make it through the day without her seeing me. Maybe I can think of something. An excuse. An alibi. *You must be crazy*, I'd say. *I was never at the lake.* And then I'd get Jessica to back me up.

Even *I* know it won't work. Hopefully I can think of something before we have class together. Before I have to face the music. I just need to avoid her until then.

But as I turn to go, she does something that makes me pause.

Her head twitches quickly. Back and forth, like she's shaking her head *no*, except it's far too fast for normal movement, so fast it's practically a blur, a terrifying glitch.

It makes my cold blood freeze even further.

Then I blink, and she's back to normal.

I try to convince myself I imagined it.

I can't.

Clutching my books to my chest, I turn and run down the hall, trying to lose myself in the crowd of kids as I make my way to class.

I swear I feel her cold blue eyes on my back every step of the way, fear dripping down my back like lake water.

When I look back—just once—she is gone.

10

Even though I don't have any classes with Rachel until after lunch, the first couple of hours of school have me so stressed out I can't sit still. All I can do is stare at the clock, waiting for an announcement to come over the intercom or for cops to rush in and grab me. Either that, or I stare out the window in the classroom door and wait to see Rachel poking her face in, pointing me out to the principal while she mouths the words:

She did it.

Waiting. All I'm doing is waiting.

By the time third period comes along my stomach is one giant knot and my skin is sticky from my constant cold sweat and I feel so gross that I'm tempted to go to the nurse and say I'm sick.

But I don't. Because that would be suspicious.

Right now it feels like everything I do is suspicious.

The way I keep looking over my shoulder.

The way I start whenever someone with dark hair walks past me.

The way I walk down the hall, skirting to the edge of crowds and intentionally avoiding the paths I know Rachel takes—especially the hall where her locker is, which is difficult since I have to pass by there to get to social studies. I can't even find it within me to bully anyone—my entire body and brain feel cold with shock.

If the cops are watching me, they'll know without a doubt that I'm guilty.

But there aren't any cops. There aren't any teachers patrolling the halls. Rachel hasn't found me.

Not yet.

Not yet.

"*There* you are!"

I scream.

I can't help it—the yelp rips from my lungs before I can stop myself, and I even drop my books to the floor in the process. Everyone in the hall stops and looks at me.

But I don't care about blowing my cover or not looking suspicious.

I've been found out.

Rachel stands in front of me. Well, she *was* standing—she immediately drops to her knees and picks up my books for me. Then she stands and holds them out.

I don't take them.

"Are you okay?" she asks. "You look like you've seen a ghost."

Maybe it's my imagination, but I swear her lips quirk in a smile when she says it. Around us, the other kids go back to heading to their next class. If they notice anything unusual, it's just that I'm talking to the girl I've spent the last year actively trying to make miserable.

I try to steady my breathing.

It doesn't work.

"I'm fine," I say, my voice squeaking.

"You don't look fine," she says, still holding the books. "Are you sure you're feeling okay? I didn't see you this morning. You forgot your lunch money. That's not like you."

She says it so sweetly, so placidly, that I feel like I'm walking into some sort of trap.

She lowers her eyes and continues to speak.

"I should probably apologize, too, for not staying around after school yesterday to get your homework. We weren't feeling too well and went home early. I hope you aren't mad."

I can't help it—my mouth gapes open in shock.

She wants to apologize to *me*?

Why is she acting like nothing happened yesterday?

Why isn't she screaming at the top of her lungs that I tried to kill her?

I keep looking around, past her, to see if there are any teachers watching us, or other suspicious adults who might be cops in disguise, recording our conversation, hoping I'll say the wrong thing and admit guilt. It feels like a setup. But I don't see anyone watching us. As far as the rest of the students around us seem to care, we are invisible. They just assume I'm going to scream at Rachel, and they don't want to be caught in the cross fire.

They couldn't be more wrong.

It's *me* expecting to face her wrath.

"Mad?" I ask. Then I swallow, try to wet my throat, which is suddenly more dry than a desert. "No, it's, um—it's okay. I did the homework myself."

"Oh," she says. "I'm sorry. You shouldn't have had to do that."

I don't know what to say.

I don't know why she's pretending.

"Are you—" I begin, and stop myself. I glance around. "Are *you* okay? After yesterday?"

Her eyes squint in confusion.

"Yesterday? What happened yesterday?"

"I just . . . I thought . . ."

I'm saved from digging myself deeper in the grave by the bell ringing. Once more, I yelp from the noise—then I'm grateful. It's a reason to leave.

Immediately, I turn to go.

But Rachel won't let me go.

"Wait," she says. I freeze, cringing from what I know is about to happen. She's going to accuse me in front of everyone. She's going to yell for the cops to jump out. She's going to—

"You forgot these."

I turn and look at the books she still holds in her hands.

My books.

I honestly forgot. Books and class are the last things on my mind.

I have no idea what's going on

         why she's here

         why she's alive

         what I should be doing.

Hastily, I grab the books from her and head down the hall.

I don't turn around.

I don't stop.

I don't look back.

It's not until I'm at my desk in the next classroom that I notice:

Rachel has left handprints on my books.

And they are dripping wet.

11

I spend the entirety of my next class thinking about what she said—and what she *didn't* say.

She was lying. Stringing me along for some sick prank. She had to be.

She said she went home early? No mention of meeting at the lake or even being there in the first place? Does she really not remember what happened? Maybe she suffered a head injury and forgot everything? But that doesn't make any sense, either, because then how did she get home? How did she last so long underwater?

And what did she mean when she said *we* weren't feeling well?

I keep reaching down to my books, feeling the covers for the damp traces of her hands, reassuring myself that I actually saw her in the hall. That it was really *her*.

If she's alive, then I didn't kill her.

If she's alive, then I'm not in trouble.

I should be relieved.

But I'm not relieved.

Every time I touch the damp handprints, chills wash over my skin. Still, I keep doing it. It lets me know I'm awake. It lets me know she's hiding something, because how on earth could her hands be wet like that? Even stranger, the water never seems to dry off. I try to wipe it. Blot it. Blow on it. But by the end of class, there are still two faint handprints on my textbooks. It makes me want to throw the books away.

I don't. But I do shove them to the bottom of my locker at lunch.

Then I look back at my locker, waiting to see the water come pouring out of the bottom.

It doesn't.

I need a reality check.

*   *   *

Rachel's at lunch, and I find myself watching her from afar.

This isn't very different from usual since we never sit anywhere near each other. I sit with Felicia and Sarah again, along with some of their friends whose names I've never cared to learn. Liz? Theresa? Skylar? I don't know and I don't care. And they seem more than happy to keep it that way—even though I'm in the group, there's more space around me than there is around the others. Like they're scared I'm going to punch them or something. I haven't hit anyone at lunch in months.

"Did you hear?" the one I think is called Skylar says. "They're doing half-priced funnel cakes at the adventure park this weekend. I can't wait!"

Sarah goes bolt still, her eyes darting to me, wondering what I'll do or say.

I barely hear the girl, though. I'm too busy trying to not think about Rachel and what happened yesterday. The low chatter of kids around me sounds far too much like the roar of waves.

"Do you know if Bradley's going?" another nameless one asks.

That makes me pay attention, even if I try not to make it obvious.

I've had a crush on Bradley since math class two years ago. I didn't tell him, of course. The only person who knows about it is Rachel, and I made her promise never to tell anyone. So far, she's kept her word. I glance over to her and wonder how long it will hold.

"No," says Felicia. "I hear he's having some of his friends out for a boat trip."

"Ugh," says maybe-Skylar. "Lucky."

"I know, I'd *kill* to go."

I'm half tempted to scream at them to stop talking about him, but the conversation quickly slides on to the next topic. I don't even pay enough attention to hear what it is. Puppies? I don't know.

I sit there and listen to them drone on and stare at Rachel from the corner of my eye. She sits at a table all by herself. If I wasn't so freaked out by her right now, I'd almost feel sorry for her. Almost. It's pretty much my fault that she has no friends, but she deserved it. I mean, who would want to be her friend anyway after what she did to me? Who could ever trust her?

It probably wasn't nice of me to spread rumors about her. But in my defense, there's no doubt anymore that she *is* really weird.

Especially now.

She sits there with three bottles of water on her lunch tray. She doesn't seem to eat any of her food—not that I can blame her—but she downs all three waters, one after another, without taking a breath in between.

Then she just sits there, one hand on each side of her tray, staring blankly at the kids at the table across from her. I look to where she's watching and feel myself blush. Bradley sits there. Along with his friends, including the mean girl Christina who started all this. The one girl I've still not really gotten back at, even though I've definitely tried.

Why is Rachel staring at them? There's a grin on her face that I don't like. Especially because she doesn't even seem to breathe.

After a few minutes, something else catches her attention. Her eyes snap up and dart around, following something I can't see. A bug? It must be a bug. We have a lot of flies around here. It's a real problem. And also why I don't eat anything with black flecks in it, even if they're supposed to be blueberries or chocolate chips. I can't trust them.

I watch her, and my fascination turns to horror when her hand snaps out, whip-fast, and she snatches whatever it was that flew by her face.

In the same, quick movement, she opens her mouth and swallows whatever it is whole.

I gasp.

And she turns her head

fast as a snake

to smile directly at me.

12

There's no escaping Rachel after lunch.

We have the rest of our classes together, and they get worse with every single minute. I sit as far away from her as I can. It doesn't help. Nothing helps.

She doesn't do anything. She doesn't say anything.

She just sits at her desk. Smiling, as if she has a secret.

Smiling, because *we* have a secret.

Sometimes she just smiles at her desk or the teacher. But more often than not, I look over and see her watching me.

Her big blue eyes watery and wide.

Her lips stretched across her face like a goblin's.

At times, she doesn't look like a girl at all, but something more monstrous, with damp, sagging skin and black-tipped fingers and pointed teeth.

Puddles form on the floor beneath her.

I can't see where the water is coming from.

I can only see her eyes:

Watching.

Watching.

No one else seems to notice she is different.

No one else seems to notice she is *wrong*.

By the time the final bell rings, I want to scream out my confession.

Anything to get her to stop staring at me.

Anything to get those big blue eyes from my imagination.

When I blink, she's there, in the darkness.

She's there, and she is waiting.

13

I practically run from my last class. I slam into at least three classmates while shoving my way to the front door, scattering their books and homework all over the hallway. They don't say anything. It's clearly not the first time I've done this to people, but it *is* the first time I've done it because I'm trying to get away. I'm practically the first out the door.

At least I'm ahead of Rachel.

I head straight home, even though I know my mom will be there demanding I sit down and do my homework immediately and goody-two-shoes Jessica will already be halfway done with hers. It's better than letting Rachel find me.

I'm not worried about her telling on me anymore.

After seeing her eat the fly, or the way her body seemed to change before my very eyes, I'm worried about what she's become.

"What's wrong with you?" Jessica calls out when I slam the front door behind me and lock it quickly. She sits at the kitchen table, homework spread out in front of her, just as expected.

"Nothing," I say, glancing out the window. I wasn't followed. At least, I think I wasn't followed. I try to calm down. Try to convince myself my heart is only beating fast because I was jogging, and not because I was freaking out over the thought that Rachel might leap out at me from behind the bushes.

"Doesn't look like nothing."

"Mind your own business, brat," I shoot back. She just rolls her eyes and goes back to her work. At least the dynamic between us hasn't changed.

I expect Mom to come in at any minute and tell me to do my homework, but she doesn't come down the stairs.

"She's in a meeting," Jessica says, noticing my look toward the steps. "And I don't think it's going well."

I swallow. I really don't want to be out in the open when Mom's done with the meeting. A small part of me almost wants her to catch me not doing my homework— at least having her blame me for *something* I'd done wrong would feel normal. The fact that everyone is acting like I haven't done anything when I've clearly done something terrible is starting to drive me insane. But the rest of me doesn't want the drama of Mom's anger. I take off my shoes and head upstairs.

I pause, briefly, outside Mom's office at the top of the steps. Her door is slightly ajar, just enough to see her legs from where she sits in her desk chair. She's clearly talking to her boss—or, rather, being yelled at by him. I can hear his voice bellowing from the speaker-phone. Her office is filled with rolls of graph paper and swatches of fabric and tile and a big computer that she does most of her drafting on. When I was younger, she would let me and Rachel come in here and play Designers—we'd sit around a big piece of graph paper and sketch out our dream home, coordinating all the colors. We made houses with giant pools in the middle and houses on stilts that were twenty stories tall and one that had an entire floor devoted exclusively to puppies.

That was before Rachel betrayed me. Before things at home started to go south and my parents started fighting. Rachel was supposed to be there for me during all of that. But she wasn't. She wasn't, and that makes me feel like it was her fault.

My breath burns in my throat. I don't want to be remembering this now.

Rachel made sure those good times were dead and buried.

Just like she should have been.

I swallow the pain and head down the hall to my room, shutting the door behind me and leaning up against it with my eyes closed.

I can't help but hope that now that I'm back in my room, things will return to normal. I'll open my eyes and it will all have been a very strange dream. But I stand there for a long time, until I hear my mom call out to Jessica, asking what she wants on her pizza because she's too tired to cook, and nothing changes.

Nothing is going to magically get better just because I want it to.

I know that for certain when I head to my desk and pull out the textbooks from my bag.

They're still sopping wet.

14

I've been in my room doing homework for all of ten minutes when Dad gets home. It's like the moment he's back, the house itself goes tense. I turn down my music. I hear Mom get off her conference call. And a few minutes later, she's stomping downstairs. I wince before the yelling even begins.

I can't even understand what they're saying to each other, but it doesn't matter. The effect is the same. I hear the bedroom door beside me slam as Jessica rushes upstairs to lock herself in her room. I can hear her crying.

I almost consider going into her room and sitting

down. I don't know what I'd say, but maybe being together would make this less miserable. I don't, though, because that would be suspicious, and even though Rachel hasn't called me out yet, I'm still not convinced she won't do just that very soon.

I put in my headphones and try to drown out their fighting. It doesn't work. Of course it doesn't work.

I can't focus on my homework, either. Instead, I crawl into my bed and hold my knees to my chest and squeeze myself into a ball. Behind my closed eyes, I can see the watery blue eyes of Rachel peering at me, her thin lips peeled into a deranged sort of smile.

For a moment, it feels like she's there, in the room, with me. Leaning over the edge of my bed. Her face inches from mine. Lake water putrefying on her breath.

I swear I even hear her laughter.

I don't open my eyes, though. I want to drown out the thoughts and the yelling. I want all of this to go away.

It's not until the doorbell rings and the pizza shows up that I get my wish.

The house goes silent.

My eyes open.

And I blink in shock.

There, at the foot of my bed, are stains.

Two wet handprints.

We don't eat dinner like a normal family. Not anymore.

Mom is eating upstairs in her office and Jessica is the only one actually at the dining table, her tablet out and a video game beeping away onscreen. Dad and I sit in the living room, silently together. Watching the news.

I *never* watch the news. It's either boring or depressing, and I don't know why anyone would willingly watch that on their own. But tonight, I need to be on the lookout. *Something* is going on around here, and I watch the local news with my pizza almost forgotten, waiting for headlines like BODY FOUND IN LOCAL LAKE or GIRL LEFT FOR DEAD, KILLER AT LARGE.

Every single headlight that passes by outside makes me jump. I'm worried that it's the cops, or worse—Rachel and her family, out there to accuse me face-to-face, because the game is now up.

That *has* to be what today was: her torturing me. Making me wonder what she's going to do next.

She's doing to me what I've done to her.

She's getting payback.

And it's working.

Dad gets up to go to the bathroom and I continue watching the news. Distracted, I take a bite of my pizza and wince as my teeth crunch through something hard and gritty. Like sand.

I look at the slice, and to my horror, there are tiny skeletons covering it, little anchovy spines littered amid piles of sand. I gag and spit out what I'd been chewing, dropping that and the slice to my plate.

When I look a second time, it's normal pizza. Normal cheese pizza. What in the world is going on?

Before Dad gets back, I get up and toss the food into the bin.

No matter how many gulps of soda I take, however, my mouth still tastes like seaweed.

I make it through an hour of news, and there's nothing.
No reports of missing kids, no Rachel sobbing
onscreen and telling the world that I pushed her and
left her for dead. Just some car robberies a few
towns over and severe thunderstorm warnings for the
weekend.

"You feeling okay, pumpkin?" Dad asks.

"What?" I ask with a jolt. "Yeah. Why?"

"It's just . . ." He waves his hand at the TV. "You're
watching the news."

I try to think fast.

"Yeah, um, it's for social studies. They want us to watch the local news and report back on it."

"Oh," he says. He almost sounds convinced. He goes back to staring at the TV, and for a moment I think maybe I dodged his question, but he keeps talking. "How is school, anyway? Do you ever hear from Rachel?"

It's like my heart squeezes in a vise. He *knows* not to talk about Rachel. Why all of a sudden is he bringing it up now? Does he know something?

"School's fine," I say.

I don't mention Rachel. I refuse.

Instead, I push myself from the sofa and start to head to my room. I'll just watch something upstairs.

Right as I pass the phone in the kitchen, it begins to ring.

"Could you get that?" Dad asks. "Probably just a telemarketer."

I don't know why we still have the landline. No one but telemarketers ever call it—I mean, come on, doesn't everyone have cell phones? I grumble and grab the phone.

"Hello?" I grunt, ready to slam the receiver back down.

The sound of static greets me.

No, not static—

it sounds like waves.

I freeze instantly.

It's definitely the sound of water.

Sloshing,

churning,

hissing water.

And over it . . . under it . . . *through it* . . . I hear her breathing.

"He-hello?" I ask again, quieter this time.

Even though I know my dad is in the other room, I feel entirely alone.

Lost at sea.

Staring down a monster.

"You've been a bad girl, Samantha," the voice on the other end says. It sounds like a girl's voice. Almost like Rachel's . . . but not.

This is raspier.

Angrier.

Lower.

When the voice speaks again, it almost sounds like there's more than one person talking through the phone.

"Bad girls always get what's coming to them."

Click.

The line goes dead.

16

"Who was that, pumpkin?" Dad calls from the living room.

His words don't register. Not at first. I stand there with the receiver to my ear, listening to the growling static on the other end and trying to figure out if I heard what I thought I heard.

It had to be Rachel.

Rachel, *threatening* me.

She *was* pretending at school when she acted like she didn't know what happened yesterday.

No—she remembers the lake. She remembers me pushing her in.

Now she's playing with me.

I slam down the phone and rush up to my room. It's only when I reach the top of the stairs that I realize I never answered my dad's question.

I close my door and press my back against it, breathing hard. Even though my bedroom is on the second floor, I fully expect to see Rachel floating outside my window, smiling maniacally, her wet hand pressed to the window. But there's nothing outside, and that almost feels worse.

She's waiting to make her move.

I just have no idea what she's waiting *for.*

Maybe I should have unplugged the phone in case she calls back. The last thing I need is for her to talk to either one of my parents. Or worse—my sister.

Jessica would go to the cops immediately, I just know it.

For a long time I stand there, slowing down my breathing, listening for the phone to ring. But all I hear is Jessica gaming away and my mom listening to music and the faint chatter of the news downstairs. No phone calls.

Maybe Rachel's given up for the night.

Maybe it wasn't Rachel at all, but someone else, someone trying to scare me.

Neither option makes much sense.

If it *was* Rachel, why not just confront me directly?

And who else but Rachel would know?

Something glints out of the corner of my eye, and I look over to my closet.

I see water

pooling

from the door.

It spreads across my carpet, staining the tan a dark beige.

As if it's alive.

As if it's coming toward me.

My heart hammers so loud it sounds like the *water* has a pulse, but that can't be possible, can it?

I can't look away.

For a moment, I consider running out the door and down the stairs and outside and not stopping. Ever. Not until I'm five towns away and this is all behind me.

Except I know that running won't work.

In my bones, I know Rachel will find me.

I remember her sketchbook, hidden under all my clothes. I jolt toward the closet and yank open the door, my feet squishing in the wet carpet. I toss aside my dirty clothes as I search for the book.

Every

single

article

of clothing

is soaked.

The clothes plop wetly behind me, making a further mess, but I don't care. My hands finally close around the sketchbook.

It's dry.

What?

I glance behind me.

The puddle is gone.

My clothes are all dry.

The carpet is dry.

I press my hand against it to make sure.

What in the world is going on?

I sink to the floor and, with shaking fingers, open the sketchbook.

It's filled with poems. Poems and sketches of girls

that look an awful lot like Rachel, only in the sketches she has angel wings and her hair falls in her eyes, manga-style. I remember sitting next to her while she was drawing these, trying out art styles, trying to improve. She was always a much better artist than I was, even though she never thought she was good enough.

I flip the page, and there's a sketch of two girls holding hands, walking away. One has angel wings. And one has a cat tail. Even though the girls are facing away, I know it's supposed to be the two of us. Whenever we would pass notes to each other, we would sign them with little doodles like this. My alter ego was a cat girl, and hers was an angel. The poem on this page, written between the two girls, right above their clasped hands, makes the breath stop in my lungs:

You were my friend
until the end.
You were the best,
but I failed your test.
Now I must try
to catch your eye

and prove to you
I'll never lie.
I'm sorry, Samantha.

For a long time I just stare at the page, until my eyes start to water and I have to wipe away my tears, even though I tell myself I'm not crying, my eyes just hurt from looking so long.

It's then I see the date at the top.

She wrote this around the time we had our fight.

Around the time everything changed.

A full year ago . . .

I flip the page. And continue flipping. My eyes skim the poems, but it's easy to see the shift.

In the later pictures, there is no longer a cat girl. No longer me. Or, if the cat girl is there, she's on the opposite side of the page, and the angel girl is watching her with tears in her eyes.

As I go, the sad poems turn more to hurt. The images are darker, filled with lightning and fire, the angel girl's wings now shaded black, or turned to bat wings. The poems are all about being picked on, about how terrible life is now that we're no longer friends.

I thought we would last
despite our past,
but you turned your back
and my world went black.

Their laughter rings,
their insults sting—
you're not there
and life's not fair.

You were my friend
and it's the end
because I failed
and life derailed.

The poems make me feel terrible. I mean, she made
me feel terrible because of what she did, but reading it
on the page is much worse than imagining it.

I pause on one page.

It's a picture of the lake.

Exactly like yesterday—Rachel sits at the end of the
dock, her black angel wings folded against her back,
sketching. Something seems off, but my heart hammers

so fast and my curiosity gets the better of me, and I check to make sure.

Yes. This is the last page. The pages behind it are blank.

This is what she had been sketching yesterday.

Before I came along.

Before I—

I flip it back, and the drawing is different.

Impossible.

Rachel no longer sits on the dock, but stands.

I'm there on the dock in front of her, cat tail curled around my feet.

"No way," I gasp.

I blink.

And the image

moves.

I watch as the drawing of me steps forward. As I jerkily shove her.

Once.

A thought bubble appears above her head, asking, Why?

I shove in response.

The thought bubble changes. *Please don't.*

A third time. *Help me!*

Then she falls into the lake.

And as I watch,

the

lake

changes.

Clear waters turn gray.

My drawn figure turns and walks away.

And as I watch faces appear in the water.

Hundreds of faces emerging,

Hundreds of hands reaching

grabbing

dragging

Rachel

down.

Until I blink again, and the page is once more serene—a clear lake, tall trees, an empty dock.

And two words, scribbled in another thought bubble, scratched into the page as if by claws:

YOU'LL PAY

17

The last thing I want to do is be near water, but an hour or so before bedtime Mom yells out that I need to take a shower.

I consider putting up a fight. But after what I've just experienced, I don't have much fight left in me. How in the world had the drawing moved like that? And the water pouring from the closet . . . Had any of that been real?

I look in the mirror when I have the door locked behind me. Peel back my eyelids. I don't know what I'm looking for—some sign that tells me I'm losing it, maybe—but I definitely don't find it. I look like my normal self. Tired but normal.

With a heavy sigh, I turn on the shower and wait for it to heat up before stepping in.

I wash my hair and close my eyes as I rinse off, letting the warm water ease the tension in my shoulders and the panic in my veins. Mom buys really nice bath products that she doesn't want us to use—my sister and I are supposed to use this gross all-in-one stuff—but I figure that I deserve to treat myself a little bit after today.

Besides, the bottles say they're for stress relief, so I think I need it.

Water pools around my feet, bubbling over my toes as I lather and scrub my skin. I keep my eyes closed to keep the soap from them, and after a little while I realize that the water isn't just over my toes like normal. It's reaching my ankles.

I rinse off my face, wondering if the tub got clogged from Jessica's hair again. When I look down, I see that the water has risen even farther. I groan in the back of my throat. I can only imagine it's a massive hairball. But

I gotta get it out. I lean over, steeling myself for the grossness of tangled hair and old conditioner, and reach toward the drain.

And something glides over my feet.

I tell myself it's just a washrag. But then it happens again.

Something cold. Something slimy.

Something *slithering* around my ankle.

I yelp and stand up, but my movement is too quick. I fall flat on my back in the tub with a painful thud.

Stars crash over my eyes and I put a hand to my head as I try to sit up.

I can't move.

Something binds me down, and when I reach for it my hands are met by cold and slippery seaweed. It wraps quickly around my chest. Around my arms and legs. Around my forehead. Pinning me to the bottom of the tub.

I gasp. Bubbles escape my lips. Water rises around me, and within seconds I can't breathe in. I struggle against the seaweed as the water fills the tub. As more cold, slippery seaweed or eels or fish squirm around me. I hold back my scream.

If I scream, I will drown.

I thrash. Water sloshes.

Surely someone will come in here. Surely someone hears me. They'll help. I just have to hold on. I just have to—

Movement!

I nearly gasp in relief as I see someone lean over the tub, their form hazy in the murky water.

Their hands reach down.

Grab my shoulders.

But they don't pull me up.

The too-cold hands pin me down, and as the face lowers and becomes recognizable, I realize who it is.

Rachel.

Her eyes glow blue, her face hangs unevenly from her sharp bony cheeks, and when she smiles her mouth is filled with thousands of needlelike teeth. She opens wide.

I scream.

And sit upright in the tub.

Shower water sprays down all around me, spiraling freely through the drain.

No seaweed. No fish.

No Rachel.

I hastily turn off the water and yank back the curtain.

The bathroom is completely empty.

What in the world just happened?

I stand on shaky legs—my back definitely still hurts from the fall, so *that* at least was real—and grab a towel from the rack. I feel like I'm going through the motions of a dream as I dry off.

Had I passed out?

Was I delusional?

It's only when I reach for the door handle that I see it.

The words scrawled in the steam on the mirror.

NOW YOU KNOW HOW IT FEELS

18

I don't know how I'm going to sleep.

I sit on my bed with my knees to my chest and stare at the nightstand where I stashed the sketchbook, long after everyone else in the house has gone to sleep. Waiting for more water to spill from the drawer.

Waiting to drown again.

The lights are out.

The waterfall never comes.

I wait.

And I wait.

And I know that this fear, this dread, is exactly what Rachel wants.

She doesn't even have to do anything anymore to torture me.

That makes the waiting worse.

19

I'm dreaming.

I know I'm dreaming because there's no way I'd come back to the lake in real life. That, and the birds in the sky aren't actually moving. They hang there, suspended, black smears against the pale blue dome, like museum pieces. Everything here is still.

I stand on the edge of the dock, my bare toes just over the edge, and stare down at the crystal-clear and mirror-smooth surface. My reflection stares back. I'm just in my pajamas, which is another clue I'm asleep, because I wouldn't be caught dead outside in these faded pink unicorn–covered things. (They were a gift from my grandma, and my mom refused to let me throw them out.) Not that there's anyone out here to see. Just me and my reflection.

I look tired. Dark circles ring my eyes.

"What am I doing here?" I whisper to myself. *Why am I not waking up?* Normally, when I realize I'm asleep, I wake up immediately. But now, nothing changes.

I wonder if maybe this means I can do whatever I want. Maybe I can fly?

I close my eyes and will myself to levitate off the docks, to soar up into the sky, and then maybe I could give myself more magical powers, like shooting lightning out of my fingers or breathing fire like a dragon. Rachel's face flashes before my mind—we used to play make-believe like that, when we were younger. Before . . .

I open my eyes. I'm still firmly on the docks.

And Rachel's face is no longer a figment of my imagination—she stares back at me from the lake, my reflection changed to hers.

I gasp and try to take a step back, but I can't move.

I look down at my legs; seaweed wraps up my calves, thick and green and slimy, like moldy ropes.

"You can't escape from me," Rachel says. Her voice is eerie. It sounds like her, but it's scratchy, deeper, like a bad recording. "You can't escape from what you've done."

She reaches her hand up, and when it touches the water's surface it stops being a reflection—it's a hand, a real hand, pale as paper and just as thin, with bits of skin peeled back to reveal gray muscle and sharp white bone.

"We will make you hurt," she says, her hand stretching farther, reaching toward my leg.

I struggle against the seaweed holding me in place. It doesn't budge, just wraps tighter, making pins and needles scream out along my legs. Why won't I wake up? Why *can't* I wake up?

Her hand claws around my ankle, ice-cold and shockingly strong. She begins to pull me down, my feet slipping on the wet, algae-covered wood.

"No, no, you can't," I gasp out.

"Why not?" she asks mockingly. "When you did the same to us?"

I blink. It has to be my imagination.

But no.

She's not alone in the water. Other faces appear. Some old, some young, in all shapes and colors. Only one thing remains the same—each of them is decayed, flesh peeling back to reveal bones and gums, their eyes wide and watery, their mouths open in screams I can't hear . . .

. . . until Rachel yanks and pulls me under with a splash, and their collective howls fill my ears with the sound of crashing waves.

20

I wake up covered in water, choking for air, gasping for breath.

I thrash against the sheets and still feel like I'm drowning, until I realize that I'm safe.

I'm in bed.

Daylight pierces through the curtains.

And I'm not covered in water. It's sweat. Just sweat.

I flop back on my pillow and stare up at the ceiling, breathing fast as a rabbit.

Downstairs, I hear my parents and Jessica talking, the faint rumble of the television. Outside there are birds and cars and people.

I'm safe. I'm safe.

"It was just a bad dream," I whisper.

I look over to my nightstand, to where I stashed her sketchbook last night. It looks perfectly normal. Perfectly dry. No wonder I'm having nightmares—I'm losing my mind.

"Samantha!" Dad calls from downstairs. "You better be getting ready for school!"

His voice makes me jump.

I close my eyes and force the last of my dream from my mind. It's Friday. Almost the weekend. And then I can avoid Rachel. I just have to get through today.

I can do this.

I can do this.

I try to get out of bed, and stumble immediately because the sheets are wrapped around my ankles. I collapse on the carpet, the sheets still tangled around my feet. At least I landed on a pillow.

"Clumsy," I mutter to myself.

I try to kick off the sheets, but they don't budge. I reach down and yank them away.

But it's no longer my sheets.

It's seaweed.

Thick ropy vines tangle around my ankles, their leaves covered in tiny snail shells and thick algae. I yelp in horror and grab at the vines. They are cold and mushy beneath my fingers, but I can't pull them away.

With every grab, they twine tighter.

With every scratch, they dig deeper.

I want to scream out, but my voice is lodged in my chest.

This can't be real.

This can't be real.

Except it is.

The sun is shining and the birds are singing and it is.

I look around, trying to find something that can free me, and find a pair of scissors sitting on my desk.

I claw my way over. The seaweed tugs me back.

Almost

there—

My fingers close around the scissors and I twist back, cutting and hacking at the seaweed until it finally—*finally*—gives way. It coils back in on itself, slinking back like an injured snake.

I scramble to my feet
        drop the scissors
                race to the door
and when I look back,
the vines are gone.
Just tangled sheets.
    Tangled, shredded sheets
        and a swiftly fading puddle of lake water.

21

Rachel's waiting for me outside the school when I arrive.

She is smiling.

"How did you sleep?" she asks. As if she knows.

Of course she knows.

I stare at her, uncertain what to say. I'm so tired I don't think my brain could put together a good insult even if I wanted to. And right now, I don't think I want to. I don't know what she's capable of.

Or maybe I *do* know what she's capable of . . .

"Fine," I say.

"You're a terrible liar," she replies, her smile

growing wider. Her hair is dripping wet. Did she just get out of a shower without drying her hair?

I'm reminded of the way the books she handed me seemed to stay wet.

Maybe she didn't shower.

Maybe she went for a swim in the lake.

"Here you go," she says. She holds out her hand. I can't see what she's holding in her fist, and I don't want to. Probably an eel or crab or some other icky thing.

I take a step back.

"What is it?" I ask.

She cocks her head to the side.

"Your lunch money, silly. I won't let you forget it again. I'd be a bad friend."

She takes my hand and forces what she's holding into my palm before closing my fingers over it. Thankfully, it's just paper. Just folded money. But she doesn't let go.

Her hands are clammy and cold.

She pulls me in closer, and there's no mistaking the scent coming off of her: like decaying seaweed. It clogs my nostrils and makes me gag.

"And we know what happens to bad friends, don't

we?" she whispers into my ear. I swear I feel my lungs fill with water as she says it.

Then she takes a step back and pats me on the shoulder. Her smile hasn't slipped at all this entire time, but now it looks even more menacing, her teeth more pointed than usual, her lips a little more thin and fishlike.

"See you around," she says.

It sounds like a curse.

22

I don't open my palm until I reach my locker. I considered throwing the money away, but something makes me hold on to it.

Fear.

The fear that Rachel would find out. The fear of what she would do to me if she did.

With shaking hands, I unfold the five-dollar bill she handed me.

There's a note inside.

I HOPE YOU CAN SWIM

I shove the money and the note to the bottom of my locker and slam it shut.

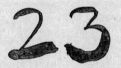

23

School feels different.

At first I think it's just my imagination, me jumping at shadows after the horrible night I'd had. But when I've taken a few steps down the main hall, it's clear that something has changed.

It doesn't take me long to figure out what it is.

A boy bumps into me as I head to my locker.

"Watch it!" I yell. I shove him back.

"You watch it!" he retorts. He turns to the friends walking with him. They erupt into laughter, and I definitely hear him say the word *loser* as they walk off.

My face goes hot.

Loser?

I think maybe it's just a freak occurrence. Some new kid who doesn't know his place.

Except then it happens again. Only a few feet from my locker, and some girl rams into me, latching on to my backpack as she goes and causing my books to spill all over the floor.

"Hey!" I yell.

But she and her friends burst into giggles.

The heat in my face reaches my eyes, and the world swims as I fight back tears.

This isn't supposed to be happening.

I gather my books and quickly wipe my eyes with the back of my hand and stand, trudging to my locker. I can't help but notice now that people are looking at me. And they aren't staring with the same fear they had before.

No.

Now they point and laugh and whisper to themselves.

As if I have a sign on my back.

As if they've learned they can finally pay me back for all the horrible things I've done to them.

Rachel.

She has to be behind this.

Before, that would have filled me with rage. Now it just scares me.

I dial the combination to my locker and open it.

The moment the door swings open, a barrage of white objects fall out from it, clattering at my feet, accompanied with the heavy stench of algae and stale water.

I yelp when I look down and realize what they are.

Fish heads.

Dozens and dozens of fish heads, their glassy eyes staring accusingly up at me.

I scream and leap back.

Right into our principal, Mr. Detmer.

"Is there a problem, Samantha?" he asks.

"I—I—" I stammer.

I look back to my locker.

No pile of fish heads at its base.

Just a book and a few crumpled sheets of paper.

I shake my head and step away from him, try to

gather my things without drawing any further attention to myself.

From the corner of my eye, I can see Rachel watching.

Smiling.

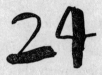

24

I manage to make it to lunch without any more strange things happening.

Well, save for the fact that people seem to go out of their way to bump into me now, and I've scattered my homework all over the tile more than once. But even those feel like blips. They are nothing compared to the true horrors I know Rachel is concocting for me.

At lunch, I know that she's devising something truly terrible.

She sits with some people that I don't think she's ever talked to in her life, her tray of food untouched before her and laughter clear on her lips. She's having the best time. Everyone around her is listening and laughing. As if she's suddenly the coolest girl in the school. Because I realize then that she's sitting with all the cool kids—the jocks and the cheerleaders and some of the really popular theater kids. Kids who were popular rather than feared, like me. People who never would have let her talk to them. Not in a million years. They barely even talked to me. They were all scared of me.

One of them, I note with shock, is Bradley. Beside him is Christina.

Rachel sits at his other side, laughing and nudging him with her shoulder. When she sees me looking at him, her grin goes so wide it nearly splits her face in two.

I immediately look away.

Instantly, the fear I'd felt from before is replaced by a new sensation: jealousy.

I've never been jealous of her. Not in my entire life.

Okay, that may be a slight lie—she definitely has nicer things than me, but that's it.

But now she's hanging with the coolest kids, including the boy I sort of have a crush on, and when I quickly look back to her, she actually has the nerve to smile and wave. She even gestures me over.

Some of the kids turn to look at me when she does, and it's clear that they're confused. Confused as to why she would want to invite me over.

Like I'm the uncool one.

Like I'm the impostor.

Just yesterday, she barely had any friends. No one knew who she was except for me. How in the world did she suddenly become friends with the coolest kids in school?

I ignore her gesture to come join them. I can't even imagine what she would have up her sleeve. There's no way it could be good. Especially since she knew I liked Bradley. I just have to hope that she hasn't told him anything.

I swallow my anger and head into the lunch line, even though I've completely lost my appetite—not that I had much of one to begin with, nervous as I was.

I don't even notice what I've piled on my plate; it's only when I've sat down beside my fake friends that I realize it's spaghetti day. Everyone's plates are piled high with noodles dusted with gritty Parmesan cheese.

As expected, they're talking about their trip to the adventure park tomorrow, working out who is going to ride with whom and when they're going to leave and come back.

"Can't you talk about something else?" I grunt, poking at my spaghetti. It doesn't even *smell* appetizing. I think they used ketchup rather than marinara.

They look at me.

"We could talk about how *someone's* a grouch," Skylar-or-maybe-Caitlyn says.

I glare daggers at her, but she doesn't seem to notice. In fact, she goes on happily talking about the trip, making side eyes at me every time she mentions just how *excited* she is to be with her *real* friends.

Finally, I can't take it anymore. I push up to standing.

"I hate all of you," I say. "You're horrible."

To my surprise, it's Felicia who speaks up.

"No, Samantha, *you're* the horrible one. I don't know why we ever put up with you. You're more of a loser than even Rachel. At least *she* knows how to be a friend."

My mouth gapes open.

Felicia knows what Rachel did to me. And no, she was never consoling about it, but at least we'd used our general dislike of Rachel to bond us together. It was about the only thing we ever had in common—hating everyone else.

For her to even *mention* being a real friend. It's just . . . just . . .

"Ugh!" I yell. I grab my tray and storm off.

Toward an empty table in the corner of the room.

It's only when I sit down that I realize this is where Rachel used to sit.

I glance her way. She's smiling at me.

Her, among her popular, cool friends.

And me, alone.

Her smile says it all:

You're finally where you're supposed to be.

I'm so busy glaring at my former friends that I don't even look at the food I shove into my mouth.

I gag.

Spit the food back on the tray.

It's not food.

It's long thin tendrils of seaweed covered in sludge, and the Parmesan is nothing but glittering fish scales.

I blink.

Wait for it to vanish, to become normal again, like the pizza I had last night.

It doesn't.

Disgusted, and before anyone else can see what's happened, I leap from my seat and throw my lunch—tray and cutlery and all—into the trash.

From across the lunch room, I hear Rachel laugh.

26

I want nothing more than to run away, to escape Rachel's torment, but Mr. Detmer patrols the halls and I know I can't leave under his watchful eye.

Which means enduring classes with Rachel.

Starting right after lunch. With gym.

Personally, I think gym after lunch is an absolutely horrible idea, since we all usually feel so gross after eating that running or doing sports is the last thing we want to do. Which is probably why the adults make us do it. I mean, gym class in general has to be their way to get back at us for being, well, kids.

I didn't eat anything for lunch.

I still feel gross.

I rush through changing into my gym clothes and try to ignore Rachel at the other end of the locker room, laughing and joking with the rest of our classmates— especially the sporty girls who have never actually spoken to Rachel before.

"You really think you can beat me?" Christina says.

She and Rachel seem to have gotten really close in the last twenty-four hours, which is ironic since she's the reason Rachel and I stopped being friends in the first place.

Rachel grins. "I know it."

Christina holds out her hand. "All right, then, you're on. If you lose, you do my homework for a week."

"And if *you* lose, I get to go on the boat with you and Bradley this weekend."

"Deal."

Rachel smiles and takes Christina's hand. I can't help but notice the glint of Rachel's skin, the water that seems to constantly drip from her. Christina doesn't seem to sense it. Either that, or she doesn't care. I have to think it's the former, which makes me wonder what sort of strange power Rachel has over everyone.

I don't know what sort of contest they were talking

about. Whatever it is, I really don't want Rachel to win. Her on a boat with Bradley and Christina and the rest? Who *knows* what sort of terrible things she'd tell them about me?

When we line up on the basketball court I notice all the stations of equipment grouped about the gym.

Oh no.

We're doing our PE trials.

A couple times a year we have to do the PE trials, which is basically the height of teacher cruelty. We're actually *graded* on how much we improve over the year, over things like how fast we climb a rope that's so frayed it gives you splinters, or how many sit-ups you can do without vomiting (again, especially horrible after lunch), or how high you can jump from standing.

They say it's to motivate us to stay active.

I think it's because they like seeing us suffer.

Our gym teacher, Mrs. Jenson, tells us the rules and points out the different stations, saying we'll have one minute at each to do our very best. I only halfheartedly listen to her explanations. I've heard them before. We've all done these before. When we were still friends, Rachel and I had teamed up and spent the entire time making jokes, causing each other to flop down halfway through sit-ups or jumping jacks in tears of laughter. Clearly, that's not the case any longer.

I am really aware of her, a few kids down from me, and the hungry smile on her face as she looks out at the gym. There's a glint in her eye that is positively devilish. Is she going to try to sabotage me here? Cut the rope while I'm climbing it or put thumbtacks behind my back while I'm doing crunches? I can't even begin to imagine what she'll dream up. It has to be horrible, for her to be so excited.

Or maybe it's because she wants to win her bet with Christina. My gut clenches. I never thought I'd want this, but I really hope Christina beats her.

Mrs. Jenson counts us off into groups. I cross my fingers and hope she doesn't group me with Rachel.

My luck is *really* bad today.

Rachel and I are grouped with two other kids, Hector and Raul. She leans forward to smile at me from down the row and even has the nerve to give me a thumbs-up.

Our group is sent over to the sit-up station first.

Hector and Raul partner up. Raul lies back and Hector kneels over Raul's knees, holding him steady.

"I'll let you go first," Rachel says sweetly to me. I grimace. I don't want to be partnered with her. I don't want her touching me. But it looks like I don't have a choice. Mrs. Jenson calls out to get ready, we're about to start. Too late to fake sick now.

I lie on the cold mat and cross my arms over my chest. Rachel settles at my feet, resting her knees on the top of my toes and placing her hands on my knees.

I jolt when she touches me.

Her hands are cold and slimy, and I can already feel water dripping down my knees.

Mrs. Jenson's whistle blows, and all thoughts of being uncomfortable fly from my head as I start to do as many sit-ups as I can. My stomach burns and my chest hurts and all I can think of is doing more, *more*, and I have to close my eyes because if I look at Rachel's smiling face I'll freak myself out and run. When Mrs. Jenson finally blows her whistle again, I flop back on the mat with a huge gasp.

Rachel squeezes my knees. Her fingers grip like iron, even though it seems like she's pretending to be friendly. I bite back a yelp of pain.

"Good job, Samantha," she says. "I hope I can do as well as you."

We switch places.

When Rachel lies back and I get up, I realize my knees are wet from her lifeless hands.

I settle in the same as she did, trying not to wince at how clammy even her knees feel—like grabbing on to damp bones—and Mrs. Jenson blows her whistle for the next group to start.

Rachel starts off normally enough. I count out loud with every sit-up.

"One, two, three—"

But as I watch, she starts going faster. And faster. So fast I can't even keep up with her anymore—she's a blur in front of me, moving so quickly that even Hector stops his own sit-ups to watch in awe.

When Mrs. Jenson blows her whistle again, Rachel sits up, not even winded, not even breaking a sweat, and smiles at me.

"How many was that?" she asks, brushing a strand of hair from her eyes.

"I don't know," I say when words finally work again. "I lost count."

"Good," she says, looking over to Christina, who is at the jumping jacks station and clearly reconsidering her bet. "I'm just *dying* to get out to the lake with my new friends."

Then she hops to her feet to go to the next test.

27

If I had any hope of Christina beating Rachel, it quickly vanishes.

After the sit-ups, we have a high jump. To see how high we can leap from standing still.

Rachel jumps four feet into the air and lands as lightly as a cat. The rest of us barely make it over one foot.

She climbs the rope up and down ten times in a minute. Her face isn't even flushed when she gets down. Of the rest of us, only Raul makes it to the top. I glance over to Christina and see her watching Rachel with shocked fascination—it's clear she's lost the bet.

Rachel's sprints are just as fast—she's practically a blur as she runs, and the sight makes me shudder. If she can run that fast in here, what chance would I ever have if she tried to chase me down? Immediately, my thoughts of just running away as far and as fast as I could vanish. She could chase me down anywhere.

And when we do push-ups, she only uses *one hand*, and she *still* beats us by a good twenty reps.

She's superhuman.

Even Mrs. Jenson looks at her strangely when the class is over. At least I'm finally not the only one.

I try to change into normal clothes as quickly as I can, but Rachel corners me.

I slam my locker door, and there she is, standing behind it fully dressed and with that terrible grin on her face.

"You'll be happy to know that I spoke with Christina. She agreed that I could bring a friend to Bradley's boat tomorrow. And I wanted to bring you."

Her words chill me colder than ice.

"I, uh—"

"You're coming, of course." She says it so sweetly. As though her words aren't dripping venom. "You don't have anything going on this weekend. Your parents aren't taking you to the adventure park, remember? Because you did so poorly on your tests?"

I can't breathe. Can't speak. I feel like I am drowning, like the air around me has turned to water and I am suffocating in the expanse.

She leans in.

"And if you *don't* come," she whispers, her breath like rotten fish. Bile rises in my throat. "I'll tell everyone about our little *accident* on Wednesday. And you wouldn't like that, would you?"

She leans back, that smile still pulled across her teeth. She takes in my blank, shocked expression.

"Great!" she exclaims. "I'll see you then. Meet at the lake at one. And don't be late."

She doesn't say the words, but I hear them anyway, laced deep within her cheer:

Don't be late . . . or else.

28

I dread our next class together.

I stand outside the classroom door as my classmates
filter in. I'm used to kids skirting around me, but now
they're making an effort to knock into me. Trying
to get back for all the mean things I've done or said to
them. A few even stare and whisper things to each other
as they pass.

Whispering about me.

Soon the hall is nearly empty. I'm going to be the
last one inside.

I don't want to go inside.

I know Rachel is already in there. Waiting for me.

Our teacher, Mrs. Kavanaugh, looks over at me from behind her desk, clearly wondering why I'm waiting outside the door.

There's no way to get out of this without being *really* suspicious.

I force down my dread and step inside.

The only seat left is next to Rachel.

She smiles when she sees my hesitation. Her perfectly sweet and perfectly innocent smile. Once more, the thought of turning around and running until I can't run anymore crosses my mind, but Mrs. Kavanaugh clears her throat and glares at me.

I've never been her favorite. Probably because I've never tried to be a good student. The only reason I'm passing this class is because Rachel does my homework. Well, *did*.

As I make my way to the empty desk, I wonder if maybe I should have tried to be good. Tried to study and learn, rather than force Rachel to do it for me. Someone sticks out their foot as I pass, making me stumble. A few kids chuckle, and the kid who did it just looks straight ahead.

If Mrs. Kavanaugh notices, she doesn't say anything.

She won't come to my aid. No one will. I am completely alone. Just like Rachel wants.

I settle in beside her and try not to flinch when she squeezes my arm in a gesture that is probably supposed to look comforting. I know it will leave a bruise.

Mrs. Kavanaugh begins the lesson immediately. I can't focus on what she's saying—I am too aware of Rachel right beside me. Even a desk away, she smells unmistakably like the lake, like seaweed, and even though I can't see it, I swear I hear a faint *drip drip drip* coming from her direction. I'm so focused on Rachel that I don't even realize Mrs. Kavanaugh has asked a question until I see movement from the corner of my eye.

I glance over to see Rachel with her hand raised straight in the air as the question registers in my mind: *What is an allegory?*

Mrs. Kavanaugh seems shocked at Rachel's boldness. Normally, Rachel stays in the back row with her head down and doesn't answer any questions. She knows that if she seems like too much of a smarty-pants or shows off in class I'll make fun of her. Well, more than I usually do.

Not that I would dream of insulting her now.

Can you insult something that's supposed to be dead?

"An allegory is when a story has a hidden meaning or represents something else entirely," Rachel says smartly.

"Right you are, Rachel," Mrs. Kavanaugh replies. "And who can tell me what a fable is?"

Again, Rachel's hand shoots straight up. No one else raises their hand, and after a moment of looking around, Mrs. Kavanaugh chooses Rachel once more.

"A fable is a short story, often with a moral."

"And a moral is?"

"A lesson," Rachel responds before Mrs. Kavanaugh can pick anyone else. She looks over to me. "Usually, fables involve children who do bad things and are taught a lesson by a stranger to change their ways."

"Correct." Mrs. Kavanaugh seems a little flustered at Rachel's quick answer. "And who can tell me—"

"A myth is like a fable, but it's longer, and often older, and it tells about the nature of life and death."

Mrs. Kavanaugh doesn't answer for a moment. She stares at Rachel, awestruck. Everyone in the classroom does.

Rachel knew the answer before Mrs. Kavanaugh

could even ask the question. Despite the heat of the room, chills race over my skin.

I can't take my eyes off Rachel. Her blue eyes gleam with an otherworldly fervor and her hands are clawed on her desk. I blink.

Her hands *are* claws on the desk. Gray flesh and blackened fingertips and long, grimy nails, water puddling in rivulets she's dug in the wood.

She catches me looking at her, and quick as a flash, her hands are in her lap. The puddles remain.

"But a myth can also mean a lie," Rachel goes on, as if talking to me alone. "Something we tell ourselves so we feel better about all the terrible things we've done. But like a fable, the heroes in myths always have to face their lies. They always have to pay for their mistakes. And they don't always make it out alive."

She tilts her head. Her lower eye rolls slightly, turning toward the desk, and the skin around her eye sags. I want to throw up.

"In fact," she says, and I swear I'm the only one who hears her words, "most of the time, they don't."

29

Every single class that Rachel and I have together goes exactly like it had in English. She answers every single question right. Oftentimes, before the teacher even asks it. It's weird. It's weirder than weird. But the worst part is that no one seems disturbed by her sudden braveness or knowledge. In fact, the teachers seem to love it. Even our classmates—the very ones who, just days earlier, pretended she didn't exist—go out of their way before or after class to talk to her. To ask her how she knows everything.

I hear her answer as I push past everyone after our

final class, history—no one makes space for me as they crowd around her desk. No one seems to notice I exist.

"You can thank Samantha for that," Rachel says when some girl asks why she's never raised her hand before. "Because of her, I've learned how to stand up for myself. I've learned that if you want something, you have to be willing to do anything—*anything*—to get it. No matter what." Rachel looks at me. "And now that I know what I want, I think I'll follow her lead and take it."

In the back of my mind, I can hear the splash of water as I shoved her into the lake.

I don't wait around to hear what else she has to say.

I run.

30

"What's wrong with you?" Jessica asks when I get in the house. She sits in the living room, a show barely watched on the TV and her phone in her hand. "You look like you've seen a ghost."

Her statement makes me pause. *Have* I seen a ghost? Is that what Rachel is now? Only, she seems solid enough. More than solid. She's more than capable of taking me down.

"It's nothing," I say. I make my way to the stairs to lock myself in my room and try to figure out a way to get out of this mess, but Jessica's voice stops me.

"Someone's been calling for you," she says from the sofa.

I pause, then turn around and stare at her.

"What?"

"Yeah. I told them to just call your cell, but they hung up. Then they called back. Like, a dozen times. You're lucky Mom's at yoga or she'd have a cow." She gestures to the house phone without looking up from her cell. "I unplugged it. Sounded like some classmate of yours pulling a prank."

"What did . . . what did they say?"

Jessica shrugs.

I take a few steps over.

"Jessica, what did they say?"

"*She* said that she hoped you could swim. Like, that's all she said. On repeat. It was creepy the first time, but then it just got annoying." She glances up at me. "You better tell whoever it is to stop calling. Mom and Dad won't be happy if it continues when they're home."

"Did she say who she was?" I ask.

"Nope—believe me, I asked," Jessica replies. She looks up from her phone then and truly looks at me. "Should I be worried?"

Of course that's what she'd ask. Should she be worried. Like she's the parent and I'm the child. She's always the smart one, the good one, and I'm the one messing up. It makes me want to scream that my little sister thinks she has to take care of me.

Normally, I would have done just that, just to put her in her place. But this is far from normal.

"No," I lie, trying to keep my voice calm. "Like you said, it's just someone pulling a stupid prank."

She nods.

I turn and head up the stairs, think that maybe if I face Rachel, maybe if I go on this boat trip, she'll leave me alone. Or at least leave my family alone. I can't imagine she'd want to hurt or involve anyone here. She always got along with my family. Heck, she was often the one trying to involve my sister in our tea parties or outdoor adventures. Rachel viewed Jessica as a sister, and I'm pretty certain Jessica wished Rachel *was* her sister in my place. I still remember the fight Jessica and I had when I learned she'd been texting Rachel behind my back, after our falling out. I'd made her swear never to speak to Rachel again.

No, Rachel never had any reason to be angry toward anyone else in my family. Just me.

I have to believe Rachel, or whatever Rachel's become, will leave them out of this.

The moment my foot hits the stair, the home phone rings again.

31

I freeze at the sound of the phone.

Jessica looks over at me. Then to the plug, which is definitely not connected to the wall.

Her wide eyes say it all:

Did we mistakenly hear that?

Are we hallucinating?

The phone rings again and I nearly jump out of my skin.

"How?" Jessica gasps.

I take a step toward the phone. I reach out, my hand shaking.

Like the phone is electrified.

Like it's a live spider.

Jessica nods at me.

I pick up the phone just as it rings a third impossible time.

"Hello?" I ask.

"You're home," Rachel says. Her voice is gravelly. "We were worried you'd decided to run."

I swallow. I *had* thought of running away. Many times. I just didn't think it would work.

"What do you want?" I ask. I try to make my words stern and commanding. Instead, they shake as much as my hand.

Rachel just laughs.

Then the phone clicks, and I swear the dial tone sounds like voices screaming underwater.

I hang up immediately.

"Who was that?" Jessica asks.

I consider lying, but my brain can't come up with something fast enough. Besides, this might be one of those rare occasions where the truth is harder to believe than any lie.

"Rachel," I reply.

"Impossible," Jessica says. She picks up the dangling phone cord. "It didn't sound like her. And how could she call when the phone is unplugged?"

"I don't know," I admit. "I think . . . I think something is wrong. Something happened to her, Jessica. I don't think . . . I don't think she's fully human. Not anymore."

I don't know why I say it. The words fall from my mouth before I can stop them, but the moment I speak I'm hit with a wave of something I didn't expect to feel—relief. Relief that I've finally told someone. Relief that maybe now I won't have to face Rachel alone. Jessica has experienced the impossible, just like I had. She has to believe me.

She has to help me figure something out. She's always been the smart one of the two of us.

For a long while she just stands there in silence. Faintly, I hear her own phone buzzing and beeping in the living room with whatever game she forgot to pause. She doesn't seem to notice. She just stares at the unplugged phone, her face blank.

Then she looks up at me.

"I don't believe you," she says.

My heart drops.

"What?"

She drops the cord and squares her shoulders to face me.

"Did you really think I'd fall for that? You haven't spoken to Rachel in over a year and now you're trying to pretend she's, what? Some sort of monster hunting you down?" She sighs in frustration. "I'm not falling for it. Whatever sort of stupid prank this is. I bet you did something to the phone and got one of your bully friends in on it. Well, it didn't work."

"But, Jessica—"

Jessica holds up her hand, cutting me off. I want to slap it away, but I can't seem to get my body to work. It is numb with shock.

"No. You're a horrible person, Samantha. I don't know why I ever thought you could be different. I'm not falling for one of your cruel pranks again. You just better hope you didn't mess up the phone, or Mom and Dad will kill you."

Before I can say anything else she stomps up the stairs to her bedroom.

Like the kids at school, she pushes into me as she passes.

Like the kids at school, I don't push back.

I stand there, staring at the unplugged phone.

My sister thinks I'm making it up. She thinks this is one more mean thing I'm trying to do to her.

I didn't ever really think she'd help me, or even know about this, but having her turn against me just hammers in the unavoidable truth:

Rachel has turned everyone against me.

Rachel has already won.

32

I'm up in my room trying to distract myself with TV when my dad gets home. I hear him ask Jessica why the phone is unplugged. She blames me. I assume he plugs it back in.

I mute my TV.

Waiting for the phone to ring.

Waiting for Rachel to continue her torment.

Silence stretches on.

I hear Dad rummaging around in the kitchen, getting ready for dinner.

I hear Mom coming in a while later from her yoga class. She comes upstairs. Starts the shower. She must be too relaxed to yell, and that feels like the only good thing that's happened today.

Downstairs, Dad starts playing music while he cooks.

Jessica watches TV. I hear sitcom laughter on repeat.

And I sit there, on my bed, the TV muted before me, waiting.

Waiting.

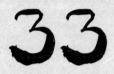

33

It feels like I blink and it's bedtime.

Probably because I spent all of dinner watching the phone from the corner of my eye. Waiting for it to ring. Trying to think up some sort of excuse to unplug it again.

It never rang.

That was worse.

The waiting was much worse. I kept expecting Jessica to mention that I'd been having someone prank-call the house. I bet she was waiting for the phone to ring just so she could prove that I was up to no good.

The fact that it doesn't ring probably only confirms

her suspicions. She probably thinks that I called the prank off. That she was right.

Even though she is terribly wrong.

I know Rachel didn't just decide to leave me alone for good.

She's biding her time.

She's making me sweat.

She probably even knows that in doing nothing, she's distancing me from the only person who might have believed me, even though it was a very small chance to begin with.

At least it had been a chance.

Now I sit in my pajamas and try to focus on the cartoon on my bedroom TV, but I can't. My body is exhausted, but my brain is in overdrive. The show I'm watching is set to low volume, just barely a hum. Background noise. Normally my parents don't let me have the TV on this late. But it's Friday night and it's not like I have to be up early to go to a theme park tomorrow or anything.

For once, though, that anger is the furthest thing from my mind. It's hard to be angry at Rachel when I'm currently terrified of her.

If anything, I'm actually a little angry at myself for letting this all happen.

I close my eyes and settle farther back into my pillows.

And that's when I hear it.

A rushing sound.

Faint, but near.

Like a running river.

I open my eyes

and yelp in shock.

Water spills from the top drawer of my nightstand like a waterfall.

I leap out of my bed, the sheets dangerously tangling my feet, and I suddenly remember waking up wrapped in seaweed. Only this isn't a dream. This is real. This is *real*. The water is freezing cold around my bare ankles, and it rushes so fast it's already covered the entire floor of my bedroom. I panic. I try to open the nightstand drawer, but it's jammed, and water continues to pour from it at increasing speed.

For a moment, I just stand there in shock.

Then I realize the water is now rising past my ankles. Shock turns to action, and I turn and slosh my way toward my bedroom door. I have to get out of here. I have to get my parents. I have to—

My door is locked.

I twist the handle, but it doesn't budge.

Panic rises like ice water in my chest while the *actual* ice water rises up past my shins. Why isn't it seeping out from the crack below my door?

It's like I've been sealed in.

Trapped.

I bang my fists on the door, but there's no response.

I yell out for my parents. Scream for Jessica.

For someone, *anyone*, to help.

I hear only the rushing water in response.

They don't hear me. Or worse, they hear me, but they don't want to help.

They probably think it's better this way.

I deserve it.

My fists hurt from pounding on the door, and the water rises to my knees, and I turn from the doorway and make my way to the window, pushing aside floating toys and teddy bears. My fingers are purpling from the cold, and they shake so hard I can barely grasp the windowsill.

I try to open it.

Just like the door, it won't budge.

I cry out in defeat and slam my fists against the window, fully intending to break it and leap out if I have to, because the water has hit my waist and it is freezing cold. So cold. I can barely breathe it's so cold. But the window doesn't break. The glass is like steel.

I grab one of my trophies and slam it hard against the window.

It bounces off like a rubber ball, sending a shock of pain up my arm. I drop it, and it splashes in the water that's now to my chest. Tears run down my cheeks as I pound at the window, hoping that someone will look up and see me, a girl with water rising about her and panic on her face. Someone passes, walking their dog.

They look up to me and wave, then continue on.

No.

I turn from the window. Make my way toward the door one last time.

I have to open it.

I have to get out of here.

Keeping my hands up above the water because I

don't want them to freeze off, I half swim, half slosh my way to the door.

Something wraps around my ankles.

Drags

me

under.

I have just enough time to yelp before I go down and water closes around me, so shockingly cold that my vision goes white for a split second before bleeding back in.

I struggle numbly against whatever is wrapped around my feet. I can just make it out in the flickering gloom.

Seaweed.

I kick my feet and wave my arms, but I can't rise up, can't get above the water that's now almost to the ceiling. My lungs scream and burn with hunger for air, but I can't get free. Can't get out.

I see the ceiling fan submerge, my entire room filled completely with water, and I know I'm doomed.

Toys and dolls float slowly around me. Suspended in freezing, clear water.

I can't feel my feet anymore. I can't feel my hands.

All I feel is the pain in my chest as the water presses in and the last of my oxygen gives out.

The light fades.

My lungs scream.

My mouth wants to open, but I keep it squeezed shut, keep it from letting in any more water even as tiny bubbles escape from my nose.

My room goes dark.

Save for countless white eyes burning in the blackness.

The countless bodies of the drowned.

I open my mouth and scream as they race toward me, scream as water fills my lungs, scream as the last bit of life leaves me.

And I jolt up in bed with a gasp.

My lungs burn and my skin is soaked with sweat. But I am alone, and my room is dry, and the cartoons on the TV babble along mindlessly.

My heart races so fast I fear it might actually shoot out of my chest.

Did that just happen?

I can't stay here. There's no way I'll fall asleep again.

I no longer feel safe. Maybe the sofa, or maybe I'll even do what I haven't done since I was a little kid and try to sleep in my parents' room. I just know I can't stay in this room a second longer.

Rachel is everywhere.

When I sidle out of bed, my feet land on paper.

I look down.

Rachel's sketchbook is open on the ground by my bed. To a new page.

A blank, waterlogged page.

Blank, save for three menacing words scrawled in thick black ink.

SWEET DREAMS, SAMANTHA

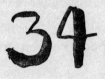

34

I don't dream again.

I don't sleep.

I sit with my back against the headboard, the sketch-book at the foot of my bed, all thoughts of trying to escape vanished. There is no escape.

I watch the sketchbook.

Wait for it to flood.

Wait for something, *anything*, to happen.

I wait until sunrise, until I hear my parents start their morning routine, until the birds are singing and it feels safe.

I know it isn't safe.

Especially because the moment I let my eyes flutter closed, just for a moment, my cell phone begins to buzz with texts.

The cell phone that I know I turned off last night.

Every text reads the same.

Every text is from Rachel, and I *know* I blocked her number months ago.

NOON. LAKE LAMONT. OR ELSE.

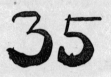

35

Jessica clearly doesn't want to speak to me when I get downstairs. She must still think I was playing a prank on her yesterday.

She stands from the table the moment I come in and heads up to her bedroom, leaving me to eat my cereal.

I feel entirely alone.

Hours drag by as I watch TV in the living room. I keep waiting for something to happen, for my phone to ring with an ominous message or for a soaking hand to burst from the TV screen. About the only excitement is the fight I hear Mom and Dad having upstairs.

Finally, a little before noon, when Dad is sitting

beside me watching a talk show, I ask him if it's okay for me to leave. I lie. Tell him I'm going to the library to do my homework.

I can see the question in his eyes—I've never gone to the library on my own before. But I also know that he knows the truth.

I don't have friends who I'm going to go hang out with in secret. Everyone I hang with is at the theme park without me.

For once, my being a bully has come in handy. He probably thinks I don't have anywhere else to go. I almost want him to prevent me from going. To say that I need to stay here where they can see me do my homework, that they have to make sure I'm not out having fun.

The look on my face probably convinces him that I'm definitely not expecting to have fun.

Maybe he's about to say no, but then Mom yells something from upstairs, and he winces.

"Sure, pumpkin," he relents. "It's probably a lot quieter there."

I swallow.

"Are you sure?"

He opens his mouth, but Mom calls out again, telling him to come up there.

"I'm sure," he says.

He slides from the sofa and heads up the stairs, leaving me alone.

I don't bother pretending to pack my bookbag. With my swimsuit on under my normal clothes, I head out the door to what feels like my own funeral.

36

Despite the sun shining in the sky and the late summer heat sticking to my skin, I feel frozen the entire walk to the lake.

It's *too* cheerful out here. The birds are too happy, the sky too blue. Well, it's blue for now. The far horizon is black with storm clouds. I keep hoping that they'll come in quickly—that way, this whole mess will get rained out.

But of course the storm doesn't come on time.

I make it through the woods and out to the lake without seeing anyone, then walk the long trail around its perimeter to reach the docks at the far end. I don't see anyone else out here or hear any music. I thought she said that this was Bradley's party? Did she trick me into coming out on my own? I don't see anyone at the docks, and there aren't any other boats on the lake.

Something is wrong.

The cold that I felt coming here is worse—goose bumps stick out all over my skin, and when I pause and look around, I realize that the world has gone silent.

Completely,

utterly

Silent.

No gentle waves lapping against the shore. No wind in the trees. No birdsong or chipmunk chatter.

And then a noise.

Splash.

Despite my every survival instinct, I step toward the lake.

Farther out, maybe twenty feet past the shoreline, is the center of the ripple. The wave spreads out toward me, lapping against the grass at my feet.

Maybe it was a fish?

Only . . .

There's something floating out there.

A log?

No . . . not a log. It's too pale. And yet colorful. I can see spots of color on it—blue and green and red—and as it floats closer, I realize that it's far too big to be a branch or a dead fish.

I want to step away, but I can't move. I'm frozen in place, staring at the whatever-it-is as it slowly floats closer to me.

And then I hear another splash, a *plop*, like someone's thrown a pebble onto the lake.

I look toward the noise and realize it's not from something falling into the lake . . . it's from something rising up from it.

Another shape surfaces, small waves rippling out.

And, like the first, even though there's no wind, it slowly makes its way toward me.

Another plop.

Another shape.

And another.

And another.

Half a dozen.

A dozen.

Too many to count.

All different colors, all different shapes.

A new set of chills races down my spine as I realize what they are. Or what I think they are. But they can't be. They can't.

I watch, transfixed, as the shapes near.

The one closest to me is only a few feet away. When it draws close to the shore, it catches on something underneath.

It rolls gently,

revealing its underside.

I gasp.

I want to scream, but the sound doesn't come out.

Fear clenches my throat. I can't speak. I can't even close my eyes as the body floats closer.

It's a kid.

My age.

His eyes are wide open and glazed white, and tiny barnacles cluster over his skin.

The colors I'd seen are from his faded Hawaiian-print shirt.

I don't recognize him.

How could I, when half of his face is covered in slime and shells?

The other shapes near.

Coming to me.

Coming *for* me.

I want to move.

I want to run far, far away.

But I can't move

as body

after

body

                    piles
                    up
                    along the shore,
                              flipping over
                              at the last moment
                              to reveal
                              faces
                              in various states of decay.
A girl in a sundress.
Twins who can't be older than five, wearing match-
ing T-shirts and shorts.
A boy in a formal suit.
And not just children, either, but older bodies.
     Men and women,
              my parents' age and my grandparents' age,
of all shapes and sizes and colors,
wearing fancy clothes or plain.

Dozens of them,
    piling
    up

at
my
feet.

And then, farther out, another shape rises to the surface.
    I know this one even before it nears.
    It is the last to reach the shore.
    The latest in the drownings.
      She floats toward me,
             face up,
             her long black hair a halo and
             her blue eyes reflecting the sky.
    Not nearly as decayed as the others.
    She almost looks peaceful.
    Except for the fear plastered on her face.
      Rachel.

37

Rachel's body thumps against another body, and silence stretches across the lake once more.

Silence and stillness and my frantic breath.

I have to get out of here. I have to—

Cold hands clamp down on my shoulders from behind, and a face with long wet black hair—I can't see her face, but I can *smell* the rot and the water—leans over to whisper in my ear.

"The dead do not forget."

Her fingers tighten.

"The dead will have their revenge."

She pushes me forward. Onto the pile of bodies.

I stumble.

Fall forward.

Finally, my vocal cords decide to work, and a scream rips from my lungs as I plunge toward the nearest bloated corpse.

I land on my hands and knees in the shallows.

The empty shallows.

I gasp and look around.

No bodies.

No corpses.

Just the wind and the birdsong and the waves lapping over my hands and knees.

I look back.

No one behind me, either.

When I bring my attention back to the water, I look down and see clouds of red twirling around my hands and knees from where I skinned them. I see my reflection staring back.

I look terrified.

Shivering, I push myself to stand up and glance around.

I should go home.

I should definitely go home.

There's no way I'm going out on the water.

No way—

"There you are!" Rachel calls out.

She jogs toward me. Coming not from the path but from deeper in the woods.

What was she doing there?

How long was she watching me?

And who—or what—put their hands on my shoulders and pushed me in?

"I thought you'd decided not to come," she says brightly. She hesitates. "But what were you doing in the water? Warming up for our swim?"

"I, um," I stammer. Water and blood drip down my fingers.

Rachel steps forward.

"Ooh, we better take care of those scrapes. I bet Bradley has a first aid kit on the boat."

Her head tilts to the side.

"We better take care of it soon. You don't want to get too much blood in the lake. It might make them . . . *hungry.*"

I don't ask what she's talking about.

I know. I already know.

As she takes me by the arm and guides me toward the docks—docks where I can now see a few kids milling about, putting things in a pontoon boat while faint music plays—I know I don't have a choice. I'm trapped.

And if I'm not careful, I'll be one of those bodies soon.

38

"Are we *boring* you?" Bradley asks.

I quickly try to cover another yawn with a bandaged hand, but it's too late. He and Christina and Mario glare at me. Rachel just looks amused.

The five of us are lounging on his boat in the middle of the lake. It's not much of a party, and it's clear they don't want me to be there, but there's not much I can do to change it at this point. Pop music blasts from his speakers, and he and the rest are laughing and drinking soda and throwing candy at one another.

Or at least they were until my yawn made them pause.

"Ugh, I should never have agreed to letting you bring her," Christina says snidely. "She hasn't said a thing; no wonder you stopped hanging out with her. I thought she was supposed to be, like, *edgy*."

"She is," Rachel says. "She's a cold-blooded *killer*."

She says it coolly, as if it's a compliment, but I know what she means. Despite the heat, I feel frozen in anticipation at her words. Is she going to tell them what I did?

Christina just rolls her eyes.

"She's boring," Christina replies. As if I'm not here at all. I really wish I wasn't here at all. "I'm surprised you even wanted her to come here. After what she said about you."

Memories try to rise to the surface, but I force them down. Of course it had to be Christina here. Her and Bradley. Mario is the only one I don't have a bad history with, but I have a feeling we're about to have a bad future.

Rachel's planning something. I know it.

And I don't want to walk into her trap. Whatever it is.

Trouble is, I know that by coming out here, I already have.

They go back to talking and laughing, and I try to

tune them out. I lie at the front of the boat and stare up at the blue sky and try to keep my breathing calm, try to enjoy this moment, even though I'm definitely trapped. There's no way to get back to shore without making a scene or jumping into the body-infested water. And there's no way Rachel just brought me out here to relax. This is about as far from relaxing as it could be.

A year ago, these kids wouldn't have looked at Rachel twice. And now they're talking and laughing like she's always been their best friend. They actually seem *impressed* by her.

"I still don't know how you were able to do so many one-handed push-ups," Mario says. "I can't even do one!"

The group laughs as he demonstrates this, trying unsuccessfully to do a push-up with only one hand.

"I guess you just have to be hungry for it," Rachel says. She looks at me when she says it, a menacing glint in her eye.

"Or you just have to want to show off!" Bradley responds, which makes Rachel look back to him with a smile.

"Speaking of showing off," Christina continues. "I think Mrs. Kavanaugh nearly choked when you answered all her questions before she could even ask them. How did you even know?"

"They were predictable," Rachel says coolly. "I guess after months of being on the outside and observing people, I've learned how to guess their behavior. Everyone is predictable once you know their traits. Once you know what someone's going to do, it's easy to beat them at their own game."

Again, that menacing grin my direction.

Again, everyone else fails to notice the dire tone.

I close my eyes and try to ignore them.

"That's so cool," Christina says. "You'll have to show me how to do that someday."

"Oh, you'll be like me sooner than you think," Rachel says.

"I hope so!" Christina replies.

I swallow what I want to say—*No, you don't. You definitely don't.*

"I bet you know everything about everyone," Bradley says.

Rachel smiles knowingly. "I know enough."

"So," Bradley continues, "you'd know everyone who has a crush on me."

My cheeks go hot immediately. I resolutely don't look over to them. I squeeze my eyes shut and hope against hope that she doesn't say anything.

Even with my eyes closed, I can feel her look my way.

"Of course I do," she says.

"Who?" he asks.

She chuckles. "I can't just *tell* you. That would be too easy. How about we have another contest?"

I open my eyes and look over.

"What sort of contest?" Mario asks.

"A swimming contest, of course," Rachel replies. She stands and points to the far shore. "If you can beat me there and back, I'll tell *all* of you who has a crush on you. I can tell you all the secrets everyone in the school is trying to hide."

"Deal!" Bradley says. The boat sways as he leaps to his feet.

I glance over just in time to see him pull off his shirt. My cheeks go hot and I look away as he and the others leap into the lake. The boat rocks ominously with the waves from their splashing. I swallow my fear and squeeze my eyes shut and wait for the rocking to pass. I know it's stupid, but it feels like the boat could tip over or capsize at any moment. Like there are creatures beneath trying to drag it down.

And there are. There are.

The boat slowly rights itself, and I let out a breath I didn't realize I was holding. Bradley and the others splash and laugh, but I don't look over to them. I keep my eyes closed. I want to pretend I'm safely on shore. My feet on solid ground.

Ideally in a desert—as far away from water as possible.

Hopefully this will all be over soon.

"What's the matter?"

I nearly jump overboard at the sound of her voice.

Rachel stands in front of me in her swimsuit, her hair lank and long around her shoulders. Even now, in the bright sun, she looks almost translucent. Slightly iridescent, like fish scales.

Otherworldly.

Terrifying.

She takes a step closer. Her shadow falls over me,

along with the scent of swamp water. "Aren't you having fun? *I'm* having fun."

Something about the way she says it makes it sound like a threat.

"Yeah," I say. "Lots of fun."

"Then you should swim with us," she says. And there's no mistaking the threat in her words this time. "Or are you scared?"

"Yeah, come on, Samantha!" Bradley calls from the water. I sit up and look out to him and the others. The fact that he's looking at me, asking me to join in, almost makes me consider it. Almost, had I not seen what was floating deep in the lake's murky depths. "The water feels great!"

Rachel kneels down by me. "You don't want to let your new friends down, do you?" she asks quietly.

"They aren't my friends," I reply.

There had been a time, once, when I'd tried to get Bradley to notice me. I'd smile at him while passing in the hall or try to sit by him during class, but he never seemed to notice. Or worse, if he did notice, he didn't care. Rachel had helped me through my disappointment.

"Oh, I'm not talking about *them*," Rachel says. She leans over the edge of the boat, resting her chin on her crossed arms and smiling down at the water. I can't help it—I follow her gaze. "I mean *them*."

And I see it then.

I see *them*.

The corpses of everyone who's drowned in the lake.

Except unlike before, they aren't just floating bodies. They shimmer beneath the water's surface, just out of full sight.

They're *moving*.

Swimming.

Their mouths are open wide, revealing rows and rows of sharp teeth, like sharks or eels. Their skeletal, webbed fingers are covered in long black talons.

The breath catches in my throat. I open my mouth to call out, because there's no mistaking it—the drowned are heading straight toward Bradley and Christina and Mario.

The drowned are going to pull them under. I push myself up. I have to call out. I have to save them—

"Shh," Rachel says. She puts a hand on my shoulder. Gently, but firm. "We don't want to scare them off."

I try to scream. I really do. But the words are caught in my throat. The breath is gone from my lungs.

One of the drowned nears the group. Grabs on to Mario's ankle.

One moment he's splashing away happily on the water's surface. The next, he's dragged under, his shocked face covered by the thrashing bodies of the drowned swarming him below. The monsters that only Rachel and I can see.

"Hey!" Bradley yelps a second later. His head bobs under briefly, and he splashes back to the surface. "No fair, Mario!" he calls out. He looks around at the water, trying to find his friend, whom he clearly thinks is messing with him. "I told you not to get my hair wet—"

Before he can finish his sentence, he's pulled under. The water froths with bubbles.

Christina swims lazily, watching the bubbles with a grin on her face.

She thinks this is a game. She thinks they're just playing.

Even when a drowned grabs her ankle and pulls at her, she splashes to the surface with a laugh. "Not funny, boys!"

She bobs under again.

The next time she thrashes to the surface, she's no longer smiling.

Her eyes are wide with panic. She splashes frantically toward us, trying to scramble closer to the boat.

"Help!" she calls out. "There's something in here! I think it's a shark!"

"There aren't any sharks here!" Rachel calls with a smile. "It must be some seaweed. Here, I'll come help you."

Rachel looks to me with a sly grin on her face. And in that moment, she doesn't look anything like the girl I once knew. Her skin is so pale I can see her skull and her sharp, pointed teeth beneath her lips. I can see her pale blue eyes behind her blinking eyelids. She is one of the drowned.

Only now she's *un*drowned.

"I was starting to get hungry," she growls to me.

Rachel leaps into the lake with barely a splash, a perfect dive.

Christina watches me with fearful eyes. Like she thinks I could help. Little does she know that I'm the reason for all of this.

A second later, she goes under with a splash.

I watch.

I wait.

Just like before, I don't make a sound.

Just like before, the water stills, becomes glassy and clear, revealing nothing but darkness.

Just like before, no one—not even Rachel—comes back to the surface.

39

I wait, staring at the water for what feels like hours but might only be seconds.

I keep waiting for the kids to splash to the surface, for this to all be some big practical joke.

But just like before, that never happens. This is no joke. This is life and death.

I'm in the middle of the lake in someone else's boat. I don't know how to get it back to the docks. And judging from the noise I hear in that direction, people are starting to show up to their boats. Right now, the lake is empty, but soon? Who knows.

I can't be out here in someone else's boat when others arrive.

They'll think I stole it.

Or worse—they'll know that Bradley and others were out in it.

They'll ask questions.

They'll think I killed Bradley and Christina and Mario.

And I did.

I did, because I didn't call out the danger.

I didn't jump in to save them.

Just like I didn't jump in to save Rachel.

I created the monster that killed them.

Guilt squirms in my stomach. Is that why she brought me out here? To see if I'd try to save them? To prove that I'm just as much of a monster as she is?

Or did she want to use it against me—if I saved them, would that mean I valued them more?

I want to be sick, and it's not from the gentle rocking of the boat.

On top of all those thoughts and realizations, I also know that the only way out of this is to swim. Through the lake of drowned bodies. Bodies that now include Bradley and the others.

I take a deep breath. Try to calm myself. The sound of a motor revving by the docks tells me I need to worry about all that later.

My first goal has to be to get out of here. Fast.

Before I can think about it too much or psych myself out, I jump into the water.

Cold slices against my skin, making the breath burst from my lips in a cloud of bubbles.

I thrash for the surface, my clothes heavy like lead, dragging me down, but I see the light up above me.

Darkness claws at my legs from below.

I keep expecting something else to scratch my ankles, for an icy hand to grab on and drag me down. But I make it to the surface without encountering any of the drowned. I look around. There's no sign of Bradley, Christina, or Mario.

There's no sight of Rachel or the drowned, either, and that fills me with dread.

My heart races in my chest, feels like it's up in my throat.

I feel like I'm swimming in the ocean with sharks

circling below me, waiting to strike.

I swim.

I swim so fast and so hard that my arms and legs burn, and my eyes burn, too, but it's only because the image of the dead kids with shark teeth and razor claws has me so afraid that tears flow from my eyes, my breath coming out in panicked sobs.

I can't see them, but I can feel them.

Below me.

Getting

even

closer.

I swim faster. The shore seems to get farther away.

My lungs burn and my arms feel like jelly, but finally, *finally*, I make it to the shore. My feet brush against mud and stone and I haul myself up to the grassy shore, collapsing the moment I'm on dry land. I lie on my back and close my eyes and try to find some warmth in the sun, try to calm my breathing.

I need to figure out what to do.

I need to tell someone. I *have* to. Even though it means Rachel will tell them what *I* did.

But that doesn't matter anymore, does it? I mean, she's

still walking around—no one will believe I killed her.

But Bradley, Mario, and Christina are gone. Rachel killed them.

Or the creature pretending to be Rachel did.

Although I know I should go to the cops, I can't bring myself to believe they'd help. I need to find adults who will believe me. Adults who know that Rachel is acting strange.

I need to talk to her parents.

Just thinking that makes my heart hurt. I haven't spoken to her parents since we stopped being friends. But I don't really have a choice. They'll be able to convince the cops that their daughter is a killer monster better than I can.

I push myself up and wobble a little when I stand— my legs still feel like jelly and my arms are noodles.

The lake stares back at me, Bradley's boat bobbing empty while new boats filled with happy families and friends start to make their way toward it.

I turn and head toward the woods before anyone can see me and connect me to the empty boat.

I don't want to have to explain what I've just seen.

I don't think I could if I tried.

46

I make it to Rachel's house without getting pulled aside by a cop, even though I keep looking over my shoulder, worried that I'll see flashing lights or the minivan of some family who saw me swimming away from an abandoned boat and chased me down.

Just like swimming across the lake, getting to Rachel's house is easy. Too easy. Why isn't she chasing after me? Why didn't she try to drown me in the lake when she had the chance?

Because she isn't done playing with you yet.

I can't help but feel like a mouse in Rachel's maze, and I'm doing exactly what she wants.

I try to take a deep breath to settle my nerves when her house comes into view. Three stories tall and filled with glittering windows, the place is huge. Especially compared to my house. The yard is perfectly manicured with little shrubs and a fountain. It fills me with dread.

What if her parents don't believe me? What if Rachel's managed to fool them as well?

It's too late to turn back now. I square my shoulders and march up the front walk—only to have the door open before I can even ring the bell.

My heart skips.

It's Rachel.

"Hello, Samantha," she says.

She's wearing a long sundress that clings to her damp skin, and her hair hangs lank and wet around her shoulders. Like she just got out of the water.

How did she get here before me?

An image of her sprinting yesterday comes to mind, and once more I'm reminded that I'm not dealing with my friend. I'm not even dealing with a human.

I don't know what I'm dealing with, other than that it is cruel and terribly strong.

"Rachel, I, um—"

"Didn't expect me to be here. I know." She smiles. Once more, I wonder if she can read my thoughts or if I'm just that bad at hiding them. She tosses a strand of wet hair over her shoulder. "But after that relaxing swim, I'm exhausted. That, and the nice meal. I thought I could use a nap."

I swallow. Did she *eat* Christina?

"I . . . Are your parents home?" The words catch in my throat. I struggle to come up with a fitting reason for me to be here. Something to make her not suspicious. I know that isn't possible. "My parents wanted to see if they, um, would like to go out to dinner next Friday."

It's a total lie and it makes no sense. The moment the words fall from my lips I know there's no way to take them back or make them convincing. I fully expect Rachel to call me on the lie.

Instead, she just chuckles.

"They aren't in."

My heart drops.

I say, "Oh, um. Maybe I'll come back later."

There's no way I'm coming back later.

Maybe I could call and hope they pick up?

"There's no need to do that, Samantha."

I hate the way she says my name. Like she knows a terrible secret. And she does. She does.

"What?"

"They are on vacation," she says smoothly. The door opens a bit wider. Something behind her catches my eye. "They won't be back for a long, long time."

Her smile grows, and when I realize what I'm seeing behind her, so, too, does my panic.

I take a step back.

"Oh," I manage to get out. "Okay, then. Well, I'll, um, I'll see you around."

Her smile splits her face in half when I stumble backward over the step and start to jog.

"Yes," she says softly. Even though she doesn't raise her voice, her words ring in my ears. "Yes, you will. Soon."

It's only when I've run a few blocks away that I feel like I can breathe. When what I saw can truly register.

Behind her, on the white carpet, were two piles of clothes, perfectly laid out as if someone were putting together an ensemble. But they weren't just clothes. They were her parents. Or what was left of them.

On the carpet beneath them were people-shaped puddles of water.

41

The last thing I want to do is go home. It doesn't feel safe. Then again, *nowhere* feels safe. Rachel could be hiding anywhere. Just the thought makes me feel like I'm being watched. I try to walk slowly through the neighborhood. I jerk at every sound or movement.

Is that color darting from behind the hedge a bird or Rachel?

Is that swaying curtain from the wind or from the monster I've unleashed?

Every single person who passes feels like Rachel in disguise. I try not to look suspiciously at everyone, but it's difficult. I feel like I'm losing my mind.

Rachel has somehow turned her parents into water.

She's somehow gotten the drowned to take our three classmates.

And those are only the ones I know about.

I don't even realize where I'm wandering until my feet stop in front of the police station.

I freeze.

Cops wander in and out, and with the birds singing in the trees, there's a part of me that knows this place should feel safe. Out of everywhere in town, this is where I'm supposed to be protected.

I imagine walking up to the front desk, asking to speak to a cop or detective. Telling them that there is a girl in my class who is no longer a girl but a monster. And then I'll have to explain how she has superhuman speed and strength, and she's drowned three kids with the help of her undead friends, and she liquefied her parents, too.

Just running through the conversation in my head tells me the absolute truth:

No one is going to believe me.

Without Rachel's parents to vouch that their daughter is no longer their daughter, what hope do I have?

At best, the police would laugh at me, thinking it's some elaborate prank.

At worst, they'd lock me up. Maybe because they're worried about me. Or maybe because—if I'm going to convince anyone of anything—I'll have to admit what happened on the docks on Wednesday. I'll have to admit that I pushed Rachel and didn't try to save her.

They'll *definitely* lock me up for that.

I turn and start walking back to my house. Shame floods me.

I'm terrified of Rachel, yes. But I'm terrified of getting into trouble for what I've done even more, and that will keep me from ever going to the authorities. I don't want to face the consequences for my actions.

In a way, I know, that makes me more of a monster than she'll ever be.

42

My parents aren't home when I get there.

"They're running errands," Jessica says when I ask
her. She's sitting in the living room watching TV, but
she's too focused on her phone to really see what's on
the screen. She barely even looked up when I came in.

"Do you know when they'll be back?" I ask.

That makes her look at me.

"No. They didn't say. Why?" Her eyebrow twitches.
"And why are you wet?"

*Because I feel safer with adults around. Because
Rachel could come here at any moment. Because I had to
swim away from monsters that ate my friends.* I feel like I

should be readying for the zombie apocalypse—assembling weapons and boarding up the windows and doors and hoarding food. But it's not like I think any of those things would actually work against whatever Rachel's become. She could break down any door and stop any weapon.

All I can do is wait to see what her next move is.

"Fell in the lake," I lie. I don't answer her other question. Just turn and start heading upstairs so I can dry off and change and figure out what to do next.

"What's going on?" Jessica asks. Her question stops me.

"What do you mean?"

She looks up over her phone. "Besides the prank calls? You've been acting really weird lately."

"How?"

"You haven't insulted me once this week, for one thing," she says. She pauses. "You're starting to act like, well, like before."

Before.

Before Rachel and I stopped being friends. Before I became a bully.

I know this is the part where I'm supposed to open up. To tell her what's going on and we will bond as sisters and everything will be right again. It's like there's this closed door between us, and all it would take for things to be right again is for me to open it. But I can't, because would she honestly believe that my ex–best friend came back from the dead and is now murdering everyone around me as revenge? She already thinks the phone call was a prank.

There's nothing I can do to convince her that what I've said is real.

But if Rachel is targeting the people close to me, maybe the only way to save her is to push Jessica away. To act like my old self.

"Don't get used to it," I mutter.

She grunts and goes back to her phone. The door between us stays firmly shut and locked.

Once I'm showered and dressed, I feel like I should be doing more. More to get ready. More to find out what Rachel is up to. For a while I just pace back and forth by my bed, trying to figure out what to do.

"What do I do?" I whisper to no one.

That's when I hear it.

Voices.

Coming from my nightstand.

I freeze and look around. Is someone in my room?

But no, I'm alone. But then—

Something thuds in my nightstand, making the lamp shake. I yelp and take a step back.

But the voices don't go away. They get louder. And they start making sense.

Help me, they whisper. *Help us!*

The voices sound like kids. And one of them, I swear, sounds like Rachel. The real Rachel.

I take a shaky step forward.

My hand wobbles on the drawer handle.

When I pull out the drawer, water spills over the edge, and the sketchbook plops wetly at my feet.

It's open to a drawing of Rachel. Rachel, trapped under the water, along with Bradley and all the other drowned people I'd seen at the lake. In shaky letters above the water's surface are the words

MAKE IT RIGHT BEFORE IT'S TOO LATE!

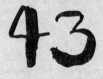

43

I sit on my bed with the soggy sketchbook in my lap.

I can't stop staring down at the picture. The details are so real. So lifelike. Almost like these kids are locked within the pages of the sketchbook.

"How do I save you?" I whisper. "How do I save anyone? How can I make it right?"

The sketch doesn't move. Nothing changes. For a moment, I feel stupid.

Then an idea strikes me.

I grab a pen from my desk and press the tip to the page.

What do I do? I write.

I don't expect anything to happen. I almost want to laugh at myself for thinking this could work. Then the ink bleeds against the page, spreading out in a smear and washing the image of the lake away.

Replacing it with a new sketch. This one of me and Rachel outside of school.

In the sketch, she stands on the steps looking forlorn, and I stand below her with tears in my eyes. My gut wrenches. I know precisely what this is, even before the voice bubbles appear on the page, saying the words we couldn't take back.

How could you? mine reads.

Samantha, I'm sorry! reads hers.

Just seeing the picture brings the memory back in a wave of sadness. I've tried to forget about this moment, have tried to turn it into something useful, like anger or hate. But seeing it again . . .

A tear falls onto the page, soaking into the paper. I rub it away with my thumb, but the moment my finger touches the page, the image changes again.

This time to Rachel in the hallway.

She's fighting with a group of girls, including Christina. They hold something above her head.

A book.

A journal.

Read it! one girl calls.

Don't! Rachel responds.

The image changes, becomes a close-up of Christina holding Rachel's journal victoriously before her. She's reading the journal entry aloud. Her words ricochet across the page. Even though it's only text, I can hear them ringing in my head like she's in the room with me.

I feel bad for Samantha. Her parents are going to get a divorce soon and I think her dad is going to lose his job. She doesn't have any friends because she's so scared of being hurt. Even her little sister doesn't like her. I'm her only friend. And sometimes I wonder if I'm just her friend because I feel bad for her. Because I know everyone feels bad for her. She's just so *sad*.

I can barely see the page anymore from the tears in my eyes. Distantly, I hear a door slam. Then the image shifts one more time.

It's a scene of the hallway. Christina tosses the journal back to Rachel. And they see me, standing farther off.

Christina is smiling.

Even your friend thinks you're pathetic,
she says to me.

Rachel is crying. But the image of me is standing there with her hands balled into fists. And even though there aren't speech or thought bubbles, I know what the drawing of me is. I know it better than anything else.

I will not *let anyone feel sorry for me!*
I'll make them *be sorry!*
I'll make all of you sorry!

That was the moment Rachel and I stopped being friends. When she revealed the truth—that she felt sorry for me, that she thought I was pathetic. And that was the moment I made the decision to never be sad or weak again.

After that, I made the life of anyone who so much as looked at me as miserable as possible. I bullied them, and I made fun of them, until everyone in the school knew that I wasn't someone to feel sorry for.

I was someone to fear.

The image fades, and with it so, too, does my sadness, replaced with an anger that has bubbled ever since that terrible day. I sniff and wipe the last of my tears on my sleeve.

"What does that have to do with making things right?" I ask the blank page. "*She's* the one who made everything wrong."

The page doesn't answer.

Downstairs, the phone begins to ring.

44

For a while, I let the phone ring, thinking that Jessica would get it before I could reach it.

Except the phone keeps ringing. Even when it most definitely should have gone to voicemail. It rings and rings, and after a solid minute I've finally had enough. I know who it will be.

I make sure to slam the sketchbook back into the nightstand. I don't want anyone else seeing those sketches. I don't want anyone else to understand my truth.

"Jessica!" I yell out when I slam open my door. Where is she? Why isn't she answering the phone?

She doesn't answer.

I make my way down the steps. I don't see her in the living room. Maybe she went out. Maybe, unlike me, she actually *has* real friends who want to spend time with her.

The phone keeps ringing.

"What?!" I grunt.

Mom would *not* appreciate me answering the phone like that. But she isn't here. No one is.

"Temper, temper," Rachel says, her voice once more gravelly, echoing like she's a dozen voices in the bottom of a well. "Anger like that will get you in trouble."

I swallow.

"What do you want?" I try to make my voice sound forceful, try to make it sound like a demand. Instead, it comes out as a quiet squeak.

"I already have what I want," Rachel-who-is-not-Rachel responds. The tone of her voice makes me shudder. She sounds . . . pleased. "At least, for the most part. The question is, do you?"

"What are you talking about?"

She giggles then, high-pitched and childlike, and the phone goes dead.

The moment it does, I hear a vibration coming from the living room. Two quick pulses, and then silence.

Slowly, filled with dread, I hang up the phone and make my way toward the noise.

It's coming from Jessica's phone on the coffee table.

I don't even have to pick it up to know that this is wrong. Jessica never goes anywhere without it—she wouldn't have left it behind if she went outside.

At least, not by her own free will.

With a trembling hand, I pick up her phone.

Instantly, an image comes onscreen.

Jessica. Looking terrified in the middle of the woods.

And behind her, with a ferocious grin, is Rachel.

45

I swear my heart stops beating.

I stare down at the photo of Jessica and Rachel, and a thousand thoughts war in my head.

What is Jessica doing there?

Where are they?

What does Rachel want with her?

But I know the answers to all those questions—I just don't want to hear them.

Rachel stole Jessica away. *That* was the door slamming I heard earlier.

Rachel took Jessica back to the woods.

Back to the lake.

And as for why Rachel would want my sister . . .

She wants me to know how it feels to be afraid.

She wants me to feel as alone as she did.

I turn off Jessica's phone and slide it into my pocket. I take deep, slow breaths even though I want to panic.

What should I do?

Should I call the cops?

Should I call my parents?

Just the thought of reaching out to Mom and Dad makes me think of what I saw in Rachel's house, the two human-shaped puddles on the ground behind her.

I can't risk my parents getting hurt.

I can't risk anyone else getting hurt over this.

It has to be me.

My nerves are electric, but I know this is what I have to do. I run upstairs and grab Rachel's sketchbook. Water drips from the edges.

As if it knows that the end is coming.

As if it knows this is the final showdown.

As if it knows I will lose.

Before I can psych myself out, I leave my home and make my way toward the monster I created,
the monster that I alone can face.

46

Scenery flies by as I run to the lake at the edge of the woods. Maybe it's adrenaline, but I barely notice the burn in my legs or the fire in my lungs. It feels like only seconds before the suburban landscape gives way to thick trees and cold, shadowed air. And then, after stumbling through the path that led me to this nightmare, I break out into the fresh air surrounding Lake Lamont.

It's empty.

Bradley's boat is still floating in the middle, and even though I *swear* there had been other families coming to the lake when I left barely an hour ago, they aren't here now.

No one is here.

Not even ducks swimming or fish splashing or birds flying through the sky.

The lake is eerily silent and still. If I thought the woods had been cold, the lake is downright freezing. The storm I'd seen earlier has drawn overhead, filling the sky with dark gray clouds that rumble with unspent thunder. And yet, it feels cold enough to snow. I'm honestly shocked that my breath doesn't come out in puffs.

Clutching the sketchbook to my chest and trying not to shiver, I follow the path out to the pier, to where I found Rachel drawing the other day. There's no one there. No boats. No nothing.

Where is she? Where are Rachel and my sister?

A terrible thought crosses my mind:

What if it's all a trick? What if Jessica is already drowned?

"I was wondering if you would show up," Rachel says from behind me. I gasp and turn around. The sight of her almost makes me scream.

Before, Rachel had looked mostly human. But that illusion is gone, replaced by the monster she has become.

She wears a sundress that sags in tatters off of her skin. Her flesh is bleached out, translucent, revealing gray muscle and sharp white bone beneath. Lank hair hangs in wet chunks down her bony shoulders, framing a face that looks like a deep-sea anglerfish—her face is shortened, widened, and her mouth splits it in two, her teeth long needles, her tongue a pale pink worm. Only her eyes retain a semblance of her former self—sky blue but glowingly so. Even in the dark gray sky, her eyes burn with an inner fire.

"Do you like my new look?" Rachel asks. She gestures to her face, and even her hands are transformed—her fingers are long and spindly and tipped with sharp black nails, and a thin webbing stretches between her talons. "I should thank you. It's all because of you."

"I'm sorry," I say. The words come out as a sob, and I realize I truly do mean it. I hold her sketchbook to my chest like a shield. Not that I think the layers of paper would stand a chance if she chose to attack me.

"Sorry?" Rachel says. "Why should you be sorry? We should be *thanking* you, Samantha. After all, if it weren't for you, we would never have become like this." She stretches her arms out to the sides and lifts her chin to the sky. "Finally, we feel strong. We feel *powerful*."

"But you're a monster," I whisper, even though I hadn't really meant to say it.

Her head snaps back to me, hair slapping against her skin. "*We're* a monster?" she hisses. She takes a step toward me, and her voice changes, once more sounds like multiple voices in one, all scrambling to crawl out from the bottom of a deep, dark well. "How dare you call us a monster when you are the monstrous one!"

"I know," I say. I take a step back. "I know, and I'm sorry. I never should have been mean to you, Rachel. I never should have—"

"What is done is done," Rachel snaps. She smiles, tilts her head like a predator examining its prey. "Rachel is no longer here, Samantha." Her voice sends chills down my spine. I take another step and feel my foot hit the edge of the pier. If I take one more step, I'll fall in. "We have devoured her. As we shall devour all who oppose us."

I try not to think of what might be waiting in the water behind me, what might be reaching out with clawed hands.

"Who . . . who are you?" I ask.

Rachel gestures to the lake with her gnarled hand. At her beckon, the surface roils, as if there are thousands of creatures trying to get out.

"We are those who lost their voices and their lives to this lake. We are the dead. The drowned. The lake is hungry. Can you not feel it? It is cursed. It has devoured so many lives and will continue to do so. But when you gave us Rachel, we found an escape. Through her, we can walk the earth once more. Through her, we can be *human*."

"What do you want?" I ask.

She reaches out and presses one long nail to my cheek.

"To be free," she says. "To feel the sun on our skin, the air in our lungs."

It doesn't sound horrible. I mean, if I had been drowned, I'd want the same thing. To be alive again. Her next words chill the thought from my mind.

"That is why you will help us," she says. "Why you will *continue* to help us. You will bring us more bodies. More hosts."

"What?"

She doesn't answer. Just smiles and points to the far edge of the lake.

And there, on the grassy shore, is Jessica. Ropes bind her tight. And behind her are three people I never thought I'd see again: Bradley, Mario, and Christina. Even from here, I can tell they're different. The sun glints off their pallid skin and their hair hangs wet. And their eyes . . . their eyes burn white.

"What are you doing to her?" I yell out. I want to run over there, but there's no way. I'm at the end of the dock and I would not only have to push past Rachel but make my way around the lake. I'd never make it.

Unless I swam.

"Don't worry," Rachel coos. "We won't hurt her. Much. She will be the next vessel. You brought us so many bodies, Samantha. So many."

"Let her go!"

"Why? You don't *care* about her. Just as you didn't care about Rachel. You wanted her gone. And you want your sister gone." She reaches her hand out and presses that bony talon to my chest. "Deep in your heart, you want *everyone* gone. That is why we were able to take over Rachel's body. She wasn't a mistake. She didn't fall in by accident. You pushed her in. You wanted her to disappear. Your will allowed us to inhabit her. You allowed us to take her away and make her our own. Your hatred allowed us in."

"No, no, it's not true," I say. But isn't it? I was so mad at Rachel that afternoon. So mad at everyone. The monster in front of me is right: I wanted everyone gone. And the lake gave me my wish.

Rachel laughs.

"It will all be over soon," she says. "First, we will take over your sister. Then we will claim the lives of everyone in this town. Everyone who wronged us. Everyone who forgot about us. Just as you wanted. We will make everyone you hated disappear. You should be grateful. You are finally getting your wish—when we are through, there will be no one left to hurt you ever again."

She cackles and stares down at the water.

There, under the placid surface, are hundreds of bodies. No longer fully human, their translucent skin and pale gray muscles sliding under the surface like eels. Eels with razor-sharp teeth and white eyes and long, spindly arms tipped with razor talons. They squirm and slip, clawing toward me. The entire lake is filled with them. So many lost souls.

So many drowned.

Rachel smiles down at them, then looks to me.

"Soon, my friends. Soon." She looks to Jessica. "Let us begin."

On the other shore, my sister screams.

47

Jessica yells my name, struggling against the monsters surrounding her. Even from here, I can see the tears in her eyes. Even from here, I can sense her fear. The monsters around her push her forward, toward the lake. Hundreds of spindly hands reach from the water, reaching for her, clawing at her ankles, and there is nothing I can do to save her. She's only a few feet from the water and a hundred feet from me.

Soon, she will go under, and the monsters will devour her.

No. They'll take over her body. She'll become one of them.

"Don't!" I yell. Resolve hardens in my chest. "It doesn't have to be like this." I hold out the sketchbook, flip it to one of the early pages, one with me and Rachel laughing and holding hands, drawn as our alter egos: me, the cat girl, and her with angel wings. "I know you're still in there, Rachel. I know there's still good inside of you." I hold the sketchbook up to the monster's face. "I'm sorry for abandoning you. But you were never forgotten. I was just hurt. I was scared. And rather than face that pain, I turned it on you. I'm sorry."

The monster's face twitches. Her eyebrows furrow and her lips tighten. As if she's fighting something within her.

She squeezes her eyes shut and her face shakes at a terrifying speed, like a video fast-forwarding, and when she pauses it's not a monster anymore but Rachel. The real Rachel.

"Samantha," she says.

I want to hug her, but I can't move. I don't trust this.

"Rachel," I whisper. "I'm so, so sorry. I never should have been so mean to you. I know you didn't mean to hurt me. I know you only wanted to be my friend."

Rachel smiles sadly. "It's okay. I forgive you. I

forgave you months ago. But, Samantha . . . this thing inside me. I can't fight it. You have to run. You have to—"

"NO!" she roars. Her face snaps, and once more she is a monster, all razor teeth and burning eyes. "No! You will not win. You cannot have Rachel back." She thrusts her arm out to the shore, to where my sister is still struggling against her captors. "Take her!"

The monstrous kids push Jessica forward. She's so close to the water, the monsters can claw at her ankles.

"No!" I scream out. I look back to the monster of Rachel. "Please. Don't hurt her. Take . . . take me instead."

The words spill from my lips before I even realize what I'm saying.

I expect the monstrous Rachel to stagger back. To vanish in a swirl of shadows. Instead, she just starts to laugh.

"Oh, Samantha," she says. "Don't try to be all heroic now. That's never been your style. Of *course* I'm going to take you. I'm going to take *both* of you."

She gestures, and on the other side of the lake, Jessica is pushed into the water with a scream and splash.

48

I scream out as Jessica gets dragged under.

"No!" I yell. I look back at Rachel. "Rachel, please! Don't do this! Fight her, Rachel. Fight her!"

The water thrashes behind us as Jessica tries to swim free. Rachel howls. For a moment, I think it's a cry of victory. Then her head twitches, and it's the old Rachel looking back.

"You have to help her!" Rachel yells. "I'll call them. You have to save—you have to—aagh!" Her head twitches, and this time she's half Rachel, half monster. "No!" she growls out, looking to the lake.

And then I realize what she meant by *call them*.

The water roils and seethes around us as the drowned creatures below flock to the pier. Bubbles and fins and talons churn from the water. On the opposite side, Jessica struggles up the shore. Bradley and the others have left her alone; they leap into the water, paddling our way with lightning speed. Paddling toward Rachel and me.

The pier shudders. Tilts. The drowned below scratch and claw at the old wood, trying to get up. Trying to drag us down. I stumble. Topple against Rachel.

"This is your fault," she growls. And then, "Hurry! There isn't much time!"

The dock shifts again. Great chunks of wood splinter away. Rachel howls and grabs for me, but I shove the sketchbook at her. She latches on to it, twists it away, but I don't let go, even though it nearly topples me.

I wait until the dock shifts again. This time, I yank the book toward me, toward the lower side of the dock, and spin out of the way just in time, releasing the sketchbook as she tumbles past me.

She yells out once. Throws the book high into the air as she plummets forward.

As she falls into the water.

I stand there, at the water's edge, looking down as she is dragged under by the drowned. As they claw at her, surround her.

The last thing I see is her face—Rachel's face, her true face. She is smiling at me.

Then the monsters swarm her, and she is carried below the water forever.

49

I don't know how long I stand there, staring down into the water's depths. Mud and silt cloud the water, obscuring everything below, but the water is still. Silent.

No one comes to the surface. Not the monsters. And not Rachel.

Moments pass, and the water ripples once. But not from a creature coming from below. No. From the tears falling from my eyes.

"I'm sorry," I whisper to the water. "But thank you for saving me. For saving us."

I feel horrible. I couldn't save her. And she sacrificed herself to save me.

The dock tilts and I jolt, expecting a monster to be dragging itself to the surface. But it's just Jessica. She shivers in the cold afternoon air and tentatively makes her way over to me, avoiding the gaping holes the monsters left in the pier. She pauses halfway toward me, leans over. Picks up the sketchbook.

"Is it . . . is it over?" she asks me.

I turn away from the place Rachel fell in and make my way to my sister.

"I don't know," I say honestly. I reach for my sister and pull her in for a hug. She is so warm against me.

For the first time in ages, I let myself cry against her.

She doesn't say anything.

We don't say anything.

Not until the sun comes out from behind the storm clouds and casts its rippling light over the lake. Jessica steps to my side, and we stare down at the lake in silence.

"I'm sorry," I finally whisper. "For everything I did to you. I'm so sorry. And I'm . . . I'm grateful you were my friend. I never said that. But you were my friend, then and always, and I'll always be thankful for that.

You never should have sacrificed yourself for me. But I'll make sure . . . I'll make sure it wasn't in vain."

Then Jessica takes my hand, and together, we turn and make our way home.

Epilogue

The entire weekend is filled with police interviews and news reporters. It hadn't taken long for word to get out that Bradley and Christina and Mario and Rachel had gone missing—once the empty boat was discovered floating in the middle of the lake, it was pretty inevitable.

Once people started investigating, they realized that Rachel's parents, too, were missing. No one quite knew what had happened. All they knew was that it had to do with the lake.

No one had linked me to the boat, though. No one had known I went out there.

I wasn't questioned because I was a suspect.

I was questioned because Rachel had once been my friend.

Thankfully, my parents had finally stopped fighting long enough to step in and tell the reporters and the cops that I didn't know anything.

Jessica remained silent—she didn't tell anyone she had been dragged to the lake. I didn't even need to bully her into it. She was smart. She knew that no one would believe that Rachel had become a monster. That Rachel had summoned hundreds of other monsters and nearly killed both of us.

No. She stayed quiet, and I kept to my story—that I had barely spoken to Rachel since we had our fight. And that, at least, was true.

Whatever I'd been speaking to since I pushed Rachel into the lake was definitely not my friend.

At least the monster was finally gone.

At noon on Monday, they call an assembly.

I sit on my own while Principal Detmer talks about what the police thought happened. About the mayor's plans to close down the lake for good. He talks about being there for each other during difficult times. Supporting each other. Being true friends.

I glance over to Felicia and Sarah, who haven't said a word to me since Friday. That's fine by me. They were never my friends in the first place.

I think of Rachel. Sacrificing herself to save me—to save everyone—even after all I'd done to her. Even after all *we'd* done to her.

She was a friend I didn't deserve.

She was more than a friend. She was a hero.

And no one here knows it. Maybe I can find a way to change that.

Maybe I can try to become a good person.

That's what Rachel would have wanted.

I go to the lake one last time after class.

I go alone. I fully expect there to be police, but there aren't. The lake is silent. CAUTION tape circles the perimeter, but I duck beneath it. Walk toward the destroyed pier. Cautiously, I make my way out to the very tip, toward the center of the lake. Toward where all the town's dirty secrets have drowned.

I clutch Rachel's sketchbook to my chest.

For a long while, I don't know what to say.

This feels like saying goodbye. Forever.

Tears fall down my cheeks, dripping softly into the lake, and for once, the place doesn't seem ominous at all. It almost seems peaceful.

I can almost imagine that this is a place Rachel would want to be.

"I want you to have this back," I say to her memory. "So you can remember . . . so you can remember the good times. Like I will. I'll miss you, Rachel. I'm sorry." I sniff. "Goodbye."

Then I toss the sketchbook as far as I can. It lands in the middle of the lake with a splash, floating on the surface.

I swallow back the rest of my tears and turn to go, picking my way carefully over the splintered wood.

When I reach the shore, I hear it.

A ripple.

A splash.

I turn around just in time to see the clawed hand rising up from the surface, dragging Rachel's sketchbook down into the watery depths.

Acknowledgments

This book wouldn't have been possible without the amazing support of the entire Scholastic Book Fair team, including the standout enthusiasm of Jana Haussmann. A huge thanks as well to my editor, David Levithan, for always knowing how to make a creepy book like this truly terrifying.

My undying (undrowning?) thanks to my parents and brother, for supporting me from the very beginning and encouraging me to follow my dream of becoming a writer (/musician, artist, aerialist, or whatever zany interest I had at the time). I couldn't have done any of this without you.

And, of course, my deepest thanks to the countless readers and teachers and parents who've reached out to share their love for these books, and often a newfound love of reading in general. Your enthusiasm has meant the world.

I look forward to scaring you again very soon . . .

About the Author

K. R. Alexander is the pseudonym for author Alex R. Kahler.

As K. R., he writes creepy middle-grade books for brave young readers. As Alex—his actual first name— he writes fantasy novels for adults and teens. In both cases, he loves writing fiction drawn from true life experiences. (But this book can't be real . . . can it?)

Alex has traveled the world collecting strange and fascinating tales, from the misty moors of Scotland to the humid jungles of Hawaii. He is always on the move, as he believes there is much more to life than what meets the eye.

You can learn more about his travels and books, including *The Collector*, *The Fear Zone*, and the books in the Scare Me series, on his website, cursedlibrary.com.

He looks forward to scaring you again . . . soon.

Be afraid. Be very afraid.
K. R. Alexander's latest is
coming to haunt you.